THE LIFEGUARD

THE LIFEGUARD

a novel

Laura Kasischke

Red Hen Press | *Pasadena, CA*

Book design by Mark E. Cull.

Library of Congress Cataloging-in-Publication Data

Names: Kasischke, Laura, 1961– author.
Title: The lifeguard: a novel / Laura Kasischke.
Description: First edition. | Pasadena, CA: Red Hen Press, 2025.
Identifiers: LCCN 2024043449 (print) | LCCN 2024043450 (ebook) |
ISBN 9781636282879 (paperback) | ISBN 9781636282886 (ebook)
Subjects: LCGFT: Novels.
Classification: LCC PS3561.A6993 L5414 2025 (print) | LCC PS3561.A6993
(ebook) | DDC 813/.54—dc23/eng/20240920
LC record available at https://lccn.loc.gov/2024043449
LC ebook record available at https://lccn.loc.gov/2024043450

The National Endowment for the Arts, the Los Angeles County Arts Commission, the Ahmanson Foundation, the Dwight Stuart Youth Fund, the Max Factor Family Foundation, the Pasadena Tournament of Roses Foundation, the Pasadena Arts & Culture Commission and the City of Pasadena Cultural Affairs Division, the City of Los Angeles Department of Cultural Affairs, the Audrey & Sydney Irmas Charitable Foundation, the Meta & George Rosenberg Foundation, the Albert and Elaine Borchard Foundation, the Adams Family Foundation, Amazon Literary Partnership, the Sam Francis Foundation, and the Mara W. Breech Foundation partially support Red Hen Press.

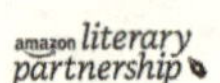

First Edition
Published by Red Hen Press
www.redhen.org

for BA—Plan A

THE LIFEGUARD

The expensive delicate ship that must have seen
Something amazing, a boy falling out of the sky . . .

—W.H. Auden, "Musée des Beaux Arts"

One

1

The lifeguard didn't notice Richie Manning, the boy drowning at the center of the pool that afternoon, under a sky so clear and blue it looked as if something transparent had been tightly stretched between Earth and outer space, like a sheet of plastic wrap pulled across a bowl of potato salad destined for a potluck.

Or like a membrane—the tympanic, the hymen.

It was the busiest day that summer at the Jolly Rogers Swim Club. All those screaming kids. All that light bouncing between those two blinding blues: the sky, the pool.

But the sky's blue had nothing in common with the blue of the pool. Every year before the swim club opened, the pool's cement basin was painted with several coats of Benjamin Moore 7055-72 (Tropical Cove Electric Aqua Blue), so it remained an otherworldly blue all summer, and the sky's blue appeared, in comparison, to be a feeble, faded pastel—the blue of paper you'd use to wrap a gift for a newborn boy: booties, a blanket, or a pair of miniature socks.

The lifeguard sat above it all, looking down from her white throne. Although she wore the polarized sunglasses required by the Jolly Rogers Swim Club, she was blinded by the blades and arrows and writhing bolts of light agitating on the surface of the water. The child-swimmers' nearly naked bodies blurred together as slender arms, sleek torsos, knobbed spines, white-soled feet until they turned into a single child, a child the lifeguard could only apprehend as a mass of instinctive energy, uncontained, and without edges.

It was Wednesday, July 16, 1969, and the lifeguard didn't notice

Richie Manning, the five-year-old drowning between the deep end and the shallow end of the pool that afternoon.

2

The lifeguard was pretty, but wasn't she *too* pretty—or at least too much of a kind of television-commercial type pretty—to be a lifeguard?

Shampoo girl. Chewing gum girl. Teenage talcum powder girl.

During the many summer afternoons Marie Manning had already spent with her sons at the pool by July, she'd had time to watch the lifeguard, who spent her shift up there in her chair stretching out her tanned legs, flipping her blond ponytail from one shoulder to the other, applying gloss to her lips from a tube she kept in a pink plastic change purse beside her while sipping from a straw that stuck out of the lid of a paper cup and appearing to be (pretending to be?) scanning the pool below her from behind her sunglasses.

Although her son had passed his Tadpole class and was now allowed to swim in the shallow end without his mother, Marie was uneasy thinking of depending on that lifeguard. Surely a girl who played the part of an actress playing the part of a lifeguard that well could not actually be a good lifeguard.

"Come on, Marie," her husband said. "Richie's a big boy now! And there's a lifeguard! You want to wait until he's thirty to let him play in the shallow end of a pool?"

"This lifeguard," Marie said. "We don't even know if she can swim."

"How did she get hired to be a lifeguard if she can't swim?" Richard asked.

"Because she *looks* like a lifeguard."

"What does that mean?"

"Well, she looks like a starlet playing the part of a lifeguard," Marie said.

"Well!" Richard said. "Tell me more!"

"Oh, you," Marie said, shaking her head at him across the kitchen table, pretending to laugh good-naturedly, if a little jealously.

Richard poured himself more wine, and a few droplets of it splashed over the rim of his glass to be absorbed into the white tablecloth to become a permanent constellation of bloodred pinpricks draped over their kitchen table for another few months before Marie threw that stained lace thing away.

Richie twirled spaghetti around the tines of his fork just the way little boys at dinner tables on TV shows did, while their younger son, Alex, sat at his highchair making crumbs out of some crackers.

"Well, go on. Please describe this beautiful terrible lifeguard to me, Marie."

Marie told Richard about the long blond hair, the tan legs, the silver whistle the girl twirled absent-mindedly all day while gazing down at the pool, wearing her sunglasses, glossing her lips, waving at the snack bar boy whenever he came out from behind the cinderblock wall that separated him from the line of children waiting for popsicles and hot dogs.

"Hmm. Impressive," Richard said. "I guess I need to visit the pool to see this lifeguard for myself. When I was there last summer it was just some lunky guy with a buzzcut."

"That was Mick Milner," Marie said.

"What happened to him?" Richard asked.

"He got drafted," Marie said.

Richard put a forkful of spaghetti in his mouth. No more would be discussed of Mick Milner that night. Marie and Richard had already had too many arguments about the draft.

"Is there more spaghetti?" he asked Marie after swallowing.

Marie said yes, stood up, took his plate, asked, "How much would you like?"

"As much as you've got. All I had for lunch was coffee."

"Oh, Richard, you need to eat lunch."

"Well, that's easier said than done." He finished the wine in his glass in a gulp. "I do have a job, you know, Marie. Such as it is."

Standing at the stove, Marie used tongs to wrestle what was left of the damp noodles out of the pot onto his plate. Through the open window over the sink, she could hear cicadas buzzing in trees, and the sound of it seemed to be amplified by the screens—a bit of tin vibrating deep inside her ear.

She returned to the table, slid the plate in front of her husband, and sat back down.

"So, Richie, is it true that this lifeguard is so pretty?" Richard asked.

Richie looked up from his plate, startled to be asked a question by his father, unsure of how to answer. Marie reached over and wiped sauce off his lower lip with her napkin.

"For instance, is she prettier than your mom? Tell me the truth," Richard said.

Richie considered this before shaking his head and saying, "No."

Richard raised his glass, which he'd refilled, and held it up to toast his son. "Well played, Richie! There's no girl prettier than a boy's mom, is there?"

"No?" Richie asked.

"Darn right, *no*," Richard said, laughing. "Trust me, you get in big trouble if you say anybody's prettier than your mom here." He pointed and winked at Marie.

Marie felt herself flush. It was so hot. So far that July the temperatures had been in the eighties nearly every day. Even after the sun set, the heat lingered. And the water she'd boiled in the pot for spaghetti noodles—Marie could feel that humidity on her forehead. She pushed her bangs away. They were damp. The earrings she'd put on when she'd heard Richard pull into the driveway after work hurt her earlobes, but she didn't want to take them off until it was time for bed. Her husband liked earrings. He liked perfume. He liked her to be wearing a dress when he got home after work. He didn't want to be married to a hausfrau like some of the wives the other salesmen were stuck with. Or, for God's sake, like some of the neighbor ladies. Jesus, Mrs. Friedlander, two doors down. No wonder her husband had dropped dead of a heart attack at forty-nine! If Richard had to wake up in the night and find Mrs. Friedlander lying beside him in bed, he'd will himself into a heart attack, too.

"Just describe this lifeguard for me, son."

Richie had to think.

"She's got a whistle," he said.

Then he thought harder.

"She has a ponytail." Richie looked up at his mother. Her bangs were a little wet. She was wearing one of her nice flower dresses and some earrings that made her earlobes turn too pink but sparkled. They had dark green stones in them, and the stones matched her eyes. Her lips were bright red from lipstick, and Richie knew that when she kissed him goodnight he might wake up with her kiss still on his forehead. Then, before breakfast, she would wipe it off with a washcloth.

She was smiling, but she did not look happy.

She was prettier than anyone had ever been.

"Well, a whistle and a ponytail and a pair of long legs," Richard said, "and I believe we have ourselves a lifeguard!"

"Not exactly," Marie said, trying not to sound too scolding.

"What more can you ask for?" Richard sighed and looked at his wife. "Not everybody has to be a great swimmer, Marie. Sometimes a lifeguard is blessed with other qualifications. And it sounds to me like Chum Rogers has found a suitable replacement for that Mick Milner in this new creature, Miss, uh, Miss . . . ?"

"Can I play in the shallow end by myself then?" Richie asked.

Despite Richard's rule against interrupting, he laughed and said, "Darn right you can play in the shallow end by yourself. You passed that Tadpole class, right?"

Richie nodded. But then he looked at his mother, who'd already told him they would have to wait until the next summer for that.

His mother was looking at her water glass, peering down into it as if there was something unpleasant at the bottom. She said, "I think we should discuss that when you get home from your business trip in a few days, Richard."

"Wait," Richard said and turned to his son. "You said you passed the class you have to pass to be able to play in the shallow end without your mom?"

"Yes?" Richie asked.

"Well, son!" Richard said. "In that case, what can we do to stop you? You're legal! Your mom doesn't want to keep you tied to her apron strings for the rest of your life, I'm sure. When a boy earns a privilege, that boy enjoys his privilege. Am I correct? Last I checked that was the American way."

Marie stood up and busied herself picking crumbs off Alex's highchair. Richie bounced in his chair, looking from his father to his mother, his mother to his father.

"Right, Marie?"

Marie tried to nod. She cleared her throat. She said, "Okay. We'll see."

Then Richard turned to his son, stuck out his hand, and said, "I do believe that I just heard your mother say 'Okay.'"

Richie looked at his father's hand until he understood that this was supposed to be a handshake, so he put out his own hand and looked at his mother as his father's large hand swallowed his.

3

The smell of coffee—hellfire and sulfured molasses—that had spilled onto the coffee maker's hot plate burned through the damp basement of the Holy Redeemer Episcopal Church, cutting straight through the mid-April underground scent of cold mud, freshly poured cement, Band-Aids soaked in mud puddles.

1990 was a year of New Rules, so smoking was now banned in the church basement, and this had caused quite a few of the other usuals to find alternative AA meetings, held in more forgiving basements.

I missed them, and I missed the haze that used to rise from them to swirl above our heads but below the ceiling's one long fluorescent light buzzing and surging from above, stirring up memories for me (and maybe for everyone else) of the hundreds of hours I'd spent under such lights in my past's classrooms. As I picked at the hole in the knee of my jeans, I was reminded of all the thready pink shreds of rubber erasers I'd left behind me after I decided—once again, and once again too late—that my answers were all wrong and that I needed to start over, but the bell was about to ring.

4

By 1969, Mission Hills is no longer a small town. It has become the second largest in the state—and, in it, there are a fair number of public pools, both indoor and outdoor, in which one can swim for free or for a very small fee. Also, there are dozens of little lakes—most famously, Crystal Lake, which, before the town had a Chamber of Commerce in charge of making Mission Hills attractive to tourists, was called, for a century, Mud Lake. And the Ottawa River cut straight through the center of Mission Hills, with plenty of places to dive off a railroad trestle or wade into the rapids from a dock. Like Crystal Lake, many people over the centuries had drowned in the Ottawa River, and every now and then someone would report seeing, from a fishing boat or a boat launch, a ghost wading out of it toward them.

Best of all, only a forty-minute drive away, there is Lake Michigan, the fifth largest lake in the world, with its long sandy beaches, its white-capped waves, its dark depths stretching out from the beach as far as the eye can see.

But the Jolly Rogers Swim Club is only a few years old, and, of course, it is a club, with dues to be paid up front, long before the summer starts. Those dues are nothing compared to the expense of the Mission Hills Country Club—to which only the wealthiest residents belong, or those who work for AmeriWay and have risen through the ranks to become managers or sold enough of what they sell (dish soap, laundry detergent, furniture polish, car wax) to be given a country club membership as a bonus.

Jolly Rogers Swim Club has no tennis courts or cocktail lounge. It's just a pool—although it is Olympic-sized, with a slide, some locker rooms, and a snack bar. There is a nicely manicured lawn that's separated from the pool area with a couple dozen lounge chairs in which mothers relax and read magazines or paperbacks and talk to each other while their children swim. There are tables with umbrellas over them.

You can bring your own lunches or buy hot dogs and chips at the snack bar.

And there is a lifeguard always on duty.

And each November, Chum Rogers, the swim club's owner, starts to run ads in the local papers and continues to do so until spring:

JOIN ME THIS SUMMER, MATIES, FOR FUN IN THE SUN!

5

After spreading peanut butter over one slice of Wonder Bread, Marie Manning placed a second slice on top, and then she began to cut off the crusts—Richie hated crusts—until she felt, before she saw, her son standing in the threshold between the living room and the kitchen, looking up at her.

"Richie, please. You're supposed to be watching your brother, not me."

"But—"

"But nothing," Marie said before he could go on to ask her, yet again, how long it would be until they left for the pool.

He asked anyway.

"Just like I've already told you ten times, I will come and get you when we're ready to go. And the more you pester me, the longer it will take." Marie pointed to the living room and said, "Go!"

She went back to the sandwich she was making, folding a sheet of waxed paper around it. She opened the lid of the picnic basket on the floor by her feet and put the sandwich on top of a thermos of Tang and two apples. On top of the sandwiches she put some chocolate chip cookies in a brown paper bag, and then she closed the lid and fastened it with its brass hook.

When she looked up again, her son was still standing in the threshold.

"Richie! What did I tell you?"

He didn't answer.

6

Those who forgave the lifeguard for not noticing the boy who was drowning in the pool that afternoon would blame that day's strange chaos.

Not only was it the middle of the week and the middle of the summer and one of the warmest days of the season (so that Jolly Rogers was enjoying its busiest day of the year, perhaps its busiest day in the four years since it opened), but that morning, three American astronauts had been launched into space in the direction of the moon.

That morning, every child in the pool had seen three American men waving goodbye to them, all at once, like fathers on their way to work. By the time Richie Manning began to drown, those astronauts were already 22,000 nautical miles away from Earth, traveling toward the moon at 12,914 feet per second. The air itself seemed electrified to those left behind. Swarms of fireflies in full sunlight were strangely blinking on and off in the branches of the trees that lined the streets of Mission Hills. The seagulls that usually circled grocery store parking lots dive-bombed shoppers who were leaving and returning to their cars. Dogs barked all day. The usually peaceful animals at the petting zoo chased their own tails before they began to attack one another and had to be chained or caged. Hospitals all across the county reported more babies born than had ever been delivered in a single day. And the awe of it all disoriented even those who were cynical, who saw the venture as a political stunt for which the wasted money had been slipped right out of the pockets of American taxpayers while billions of humans across the globe starved—as well as those who'd been superstitious. ("This will not end well.") And those who'd been skeptical. ("It's a sham: sure, they're going to walk on the moon, but the moon they'll be walking on is waiting for them in a television studio in Los Angeles.") And even those who foresaw divine retribution. ("The moon was not meant to be walked on. Remember the Tower of Babel? Misfortune will follow—fires, floods, violence in the street. The war in Vietnam will be lost.")

What they all had in common, by mid-afternoon, was that when they looked up and saw the sky, it looked different than it had the day before.

Still, those who blamed the lifeguard made no excuses for her. They asked why she hadn't been prepared for this. Of all the days a lifeguard needed to watch a swimming pool full of children most carefully was the very day she hadn't. But she'd managed to wear lip gloss, hadn't she? She'd brushed her blond hair. She'd oiled her legs with Hawaiian Tropic and managed, as always, to dangle those legs for all to see from her white throne above the pool. She'd even worn tiny silver doves in her pierced ears and a silver chain around her neck. She'd eaten a grilled cheese sandwich at the swim club snack bar, and she'd sipped a vanilla milkshake from a paper cup with a straw.

All of this was reported, by those who'd been at the pool, to the newspaper.

And all of this she managed to do while failing to notice the boy who was drowning in plain sight right below her at the center of the pool.

7

Long after so much else had been forgotten, Becca Brummler would recall the thrill and chaos of the swim club to which she'd belonged for half of one strange summer of the ninth year of her life.

Jolly Rogers.

Becca hadn't known then that a Jolly Roger was the name of a type of flag flown from the masts of pirate ships. A decade later, in college, her professor of History 101 would stand in front of a screen onto which he'd projected a slide of the Union Jack—all its bright blues and reds and whites in stripes—and say, waving his hands around in the air as if creating an image for them to see cast over the image on the screen:

"So, you're a British sailor who's been at sea for weeks without seeing anything but water. Suddenly you spy a ship sailing in your direction, and it's flying the Union Jack. You might be out of fresh water or whiskey or beer. You'd be happy, right? Company! Assistance! So, what would you do? You'd haul sail and move your ship toward your compatriots as quickly as the wind would take you.

"But now imagine that, once you've sailed within shouting range of that ship, after it's too late to turn back, that ship pulls down the Union Jack and hoists—"

The professor nodded to his teaching assistant at the slide projector, and the Union Jack was replaced with a black flag bearing a hollow-eyed skull with two crossbones, and a few students gasped, as if they'd encountered this before and it hadn't ended well.

"Behold! The Jolly Roger!"

8

Maybe, Richie thought, the lifeguard was as pretty as his prettiest babysitter:

Nicole from Down the Street.

Except that the lifeguard was much stricter than Nicole, who would let you eat your SpaghettiOs in the living room with your bowl on the floor while you lay on your stomach and you could watch whatever you wanted on TV for as long as you wanted—*just don't spill anything on the carpet or on the couch, okay, and don't tell your mom.*

Yes, the lifeguard was just as pretty as his favorite babysitter, but the lifeguard was nothing like Nicole from Down the Street. Richie had witnessed, on a number of occasions, boys just a little older than himself being yelled at by that lifeguard:

"Get out! Get out of the pool! *You're suspended.*"

Suspended meant, it seemed, that you could not get back in the pool.

Which was the worst thing Richie could imagine.

And he also didn't know how long *suspended* lasted.

All day? *Forever?*

He never wanted to find out!

He'd never seen a girl be suspended. The girls old enough to be without an adult with them in the pool just swam and squealed. They never jumped on each other's backs or held each other underwater like the boys.

The boys at whom the lifeguard shouted would either look up at the lifeguard with very angry expressions on their faces, or they would look away and cry. Sometimes the boy's mother would come hurrying up and out of a lounge chair, banging through the gate. She would yank at that boy's arm, swat him on the butt, say something about *Out Right Now.* It was the worst thing that had ever happened to any boy.

So when Richie thought about the lifeguard, he didn't think about her as pretty. He thought about how one day he would be an older boy and she would blow her whistle at him. He thought about how she was always up there, watching and watching, and how he never wanted to know what it felt like to be told to leave the pool (*for how long?*) and to be separated from everyone else (*forever?*).

To be led away by your mother, by your arm.

Your mother!

You loved her so much, and she was angry at you, pulling your arm while you could still hear the others in the pool behind you, how they just went on with their splashing and laughing as if you'd never been there, so you weren't even gone.

9

Before she left for the pool that day, after watching the Apollo launch with her mother, the lifeguard went upstairs, tied her hair back into a ponytail, applied gloss to her lips, slid the posts of two silver doves into her earlobes, put on her black swimsuit, and came back down into the living room with a shoestring.

The straps of her swimsuit had to be tied together in the back or they would, maddeningly and unsafely, slip down her shoulders all day. The lifeguard was thin-framed, but tall, with B-cup breasts, but there were only three sizes of Jolly Rogers lifeguard swimsuits to choose from: small, medium, large. She was none of these sizes, so the suit that fit the length of her torso and the size of her breasts had straps that were too loose to be held up by her shoulders.

By July, the lifeguard's mother didn't need to be asked. She took the shoestring from her daughter and stood behind her to loop it through the straps and tie it in a bow (not a knot, in case the lifeguard needed to loosen it quickly) between her shoulder blades. She was able to line that pale shoestring up precisely with the tan lines on the lifeguard's bronze back with its downy scattering of light blonde hairs.

When her mother was done tying the straps, the lifeguard slipped her thumb under one of them to slide it over her shoulder bone snugly and center the swim suit's skull and cross bones logo over her heart.

"Be careful driving, sweetheart."

She handed the lifeguard the car keys.

The lifeguard could have ridden her bike, but her mother preferred her to drive. It seemed safer, especially since a boy from the lifeguard's high school had, on his way to work at Jersey Junction Ice Cream Parlor, been hit by a car a few weeks earlier. It was good to be surrounded by metal, cushioned by upholstery when something hit. The boy was fine, but he might not have been.

And although Mission Hills was still a medium-sized city, it was getting larger. Things happened to teenage girls like the lifeguard in medium-sized cities, even in the safest sections of them—especially pretty girls like her daughter, good girls who were just walking down the street with their purses, which might be found later tossed into vacant fields.

The world was changing. It was important to stay safe. The lifeguard's dead father would have wanted their daughter to take the car to work, even if it was more expensive, even if the pool could be biked to in under twenty minutes.

The lifeguard smiled and shrugged off another suggestion that she should eat some breakfast before leaving, saying once again that she'd get a grilled cheese sandwich and a milkshake at the snack bar (where food was free for lifeguards) and that she was going to be late if she didn't hurry.

She kissed her mother's cheek.

After the screen door slapped shut, the lifeguard's mother watched her daughter back the Duster, coughing like an old man, out of the garage, into the driveway, and she stayed standing there to watch her daughter maneuver the rusty thing into the street, drive a few feet to the end of their block, stop at the sign, and turn (right) in the direction of the Jolly Rogers Swim Club.

Before she stepped away from the door, to return to the television set—on which Walter Cronkite was still framed, fuzzy and gray, moving his lips—the lifeguard's mother watched as a little girl rode her bike down the sidewalk across the street. She was standing on the pedals with her long red hair flying behind her.

The bike was too big for that little girl.

The long red hair was like a banner or a torch being borne through the neighborhood.

The bike was pretty—pale blue with a white wicker basket between its handles, out of which a flowered beach towel flapped.

The bike wobbled.

Seeing this, the lifeguard's mother gasped.

That little girl couldn't get her bottom to the white seat and pedal at the same time. Still, she didn't topple over. By God, she just kept pedaling with all her strength, moving faster. Her chin was jutted out stubbornly, hands wrapped around the white rubber grips. To the lifeguard's mother it looked pitiful, but also admirable. She was reminded of a thing she'd once seen at the beach, back when she'd lived in Texas with her dead husband: a crab wrestling for its life with a seagull. The lifeguard's mother had stood up from the towel she'd been lying on, her feet burning on the hot sand. She'd been about to take a step toward the two of them, to scare the seagull enough for it to drop the crab from its beak, before she stopped herself, realizing she had no idea which of these creatures most deserved to win the fight.

So, instead of intervening, she just watched until the seagull gave up on its own, too weak, or not hungry enough, to win, flying off into the sky above the Gulf of Mexico, screaming obscenities, while the crab scrabbled sideways into a hole it quickly dug for itself in the wet sand.

At the end of the block the little girl on the bike turned the same corner her daughter had turned—also in the direction of the Jolly Rogers Swim Club—and then the lifeguard's mother closed the door.

10

I hoped I didn't look as sickly as the others did under that fluorescent light in the basement of Holy Redeemer. I hoped I didn't look as hungover as I felt. I hoped I didn't still smell like chardonnay or cabernet or whatever drugstore bottle of French wine I'd ended the night before this meeting drinking.

And I hoped the moderator, Steve, wouldn't call on me, since I wasn't sure whether or not, if I tried to answer a question, anything other than a staticky crackle—the sound of a radio set between stations—would come out of my mouth.

Usually Steve just let those of us who seemed to prefer to sit in silence do so. But he was also clearly uncomfortable with silence. So when too much of that went on too long he'd start to clear his throat a lot, and then he'd look around the circle and stare at each of us until someone accidentally met his eyes, and then that person would generally feel the need to say something.

I'd usually been happy enough to speak up before this. I liked to please Steve. He was in his fifties. Shaved head. Gray goatee. I'd never seen him wear anything but flannel shirts. I imagined he worked outdoors—felling trees, forging trails, hacking paths through the dark woods of New Hampshire to connect one razed place to another. His face looked like it was made of rawhide. I tried not to believe that I had a crush on him, but I knew did. I loved to amuse him when I said, "Well, I'm happy to say I've been sober now for a year, three months, a week, and two days, as of—" I'd look at my wrist watch then and say, "—about an hour ago?"

Steve would smile. I'd note a few discolored teeth.

I'd hoped it might be too lively an evening to get a word in edgewise, or at least to have it noted that I was being strangely silent; however, there were fewer than a dozen of us in attendance, and no one seemed to have much to say. I avoided his eyes by picking away the soft threads bared at the hole in the knee of my jeans, but after only half an hour I'd managed to pick away enough to exhume my entire kneecap through that hole, after which I was both horrified and unsurprised to find on it a moist scab forming over a fresh abrasion.

What had I done?

Then:

"Sarah? How are you doing? Anything you'd like to share? You haven't had much to say."

The room was quiet.

I had to look up.

The room was all eyes, and the eyes radiated a consolidated, steady beam of exhausted interest in my direction.

Such compassionate curiosity!

I shook my head.

These alcoholics were wretched. I hated all of them. And I had no interest in confessing my sins to them. They could wait for days to hear my answer to Steve's question if they had nothing to do but stare at me.

However, I knew, only too well, that they *would* wait.

All those eyes.

I could've seen my reflection in them if I'd stared back, I thought.

If I stared *too* long, I could have glimpsed my future in them—which was something I did not wish to see. So instead I looked up at the ceiling into the fluorescence overhead until that long bulb surged (shorting out?) and dimmed before it resumed its unwavering glare.

I cleared my throat. I smiled. I said, "Well, I'm sorry for the silence, but I have a helluva hangover."

Before I understood that the tone of my voice made this statement sound like a challenge, I'd already spoken in that tone.

Shit.

I'd wanted to sound chagrinned at least. Or helpless. Hopeless. Ashamed or forlorn, not *proud.*

But when I looked around the circle, no one even looked surprised, let alone affronted. All those eyes seemed to have floated away from their faces, hovering in the chilled basement air, inching closer, like the eyes of animals in a petting zoo or at night coming out of the shadows—sad and shy.

These people were strangers to me. They knew nothing whatsoever about me. All they knew was my first name, which wasn't my real first name. Most of them knew from previous meetings that I'd moved to town a few months earlier, after an unfortunate incident in Chicago, the nature of which ("for legal reasons") I could not yet reveal to them (and never would)—and, of course, that I was an alcoholic.

Still, they seemed to care about me. Jesus. Their benevolence made me feel far sorrier for them than I could feel for myself.

I felt that the kindest thing I could do for them would be to sound as unrepentant as possible.

If I didn't want their help or understanding, it would set them free. They could go home, drink their herbal teas and feel superior about the choices they were making and the commitments they were keeping and all the self-care they managed to give themselves while gritting their teeth through one long day at a time. They would not have to face what they actually were: cast-off, set adrift, having been banned by themselves from every cozy bar, every wild party, every toast to the bride and groom that had been, until it was over, the happiest parts of their existence.

"Thanks," I said, "but I don't need all this lovely pity. I don't need any of it."

Two

10

A letter arrived in the mail in the middle of January, delivered to the front door by Mr. George, their mailman. It was a Saturday, so Richie was the one to go to the door to get the mail. He was always excited to hear Mr. George's boots stomp up the stairs to their front porch, to see the snow on his hat and his red cheeks. He didn't even have time to slide the mail through the slot because Richie was already there to take the envelopes from him.

"Here you go, Squirt," Mr. George said, handing over four envelopes. On the upper left hand corner of the envelope on top there was a cartoon of a pirate—striped shirt, peg leg, a patch over his eye, a bushy mustache.

As soon as Richie saw this, it all came back to him in a flash, but also slowly, as though it was swimming toward him out of some other five-year-old's memory:

The pool. That blue. Last summer. Aqua blue.

That's what his mother had called it.

And the sweet smell of the water. And the sting of it in his nose and eyes.

But since it was Saturday, his father was home. He came out of the kitchen and into the living room holding out his hand for the mail. Richie did not want to give the envelope with the pirate on it to his father because he remembered something else, dimly, from the past, about the pool. An argument. How expensive the dues were, and how *for God's sake, Marie, how many times last summer did you actually go to that pool? Chum Rogers might as well be minting his own money. If you're not going to go more than once a week again next summer, we aren't going to pay that kind of money to belong to a club.*

Richie remembered his mother saying something that made his heart start to pound hard in his chest: "Fine, Richard, I never thought we could afford it anyway. You were the one who—"

"Marie, who could possibly afford this kind of thing on my pittance—with two kids and a leaky roof? Maybe if I worked for—"

"You're right," his mother had said. "There's the roof, and also—"

His father laughed then, but not as if he'd heard something funny. He said, "The roof, Marie? Please! Just forget about the *roof*! The swim club dues won't even make a dent in *that* kind of expense. Just join your club again. All I'm asking—and I don't think it's too much to ask, since it's not like I'm making a king's ransom—is that you try to go more often next summer than you did last summer so that Chum Rogers isn't just robbing us blind."

After he took the mail from Richie, his father looked at the envelopes and then left them on the kitchen table. If he said anything about the pool to Richie's mother after that, Richie didn't hear it, and a few days later she put a check in an envelope and licked the flap of it. She opened a drawer and took out a roll of stamps, which were like the stickers you got after going to the dentist, but which were worth money, so that even though Richie wanted to keep one with an American flag on it, he couldn't.

She licked the stamp and put it at the edge of the envelope, and then she asked him, "Do you remember going to the pool last summer, Richie?"

Richie shrugged, as if he wasn't sure, because he still felt afraid that something could happen and that there would be no pool again. He was afraid to admit he remembered.

But he did.

Now, it was winter, and it had been winter for almost forever since the pool. And in winter his days were mostly made from the long dark hallway of West Mission Elementary School, at the end of which there were orange double doors and a light (sometimes gray and sometimes blinding white) bouncing off the snow from the sky. The hallway was cluttered with red rubber and fat black boots standing in small puddles of melted snow. In his classroom they wore sneakers, and it was warm (sometimes so warm he could hardly breathe—everything turning to dust blowing up out of the grills in the heaters that were under the windows) so that he would, inside, forget for a while about winter and boots, especially when it was so cold out that recess was in the gym instead of on the playground, so that the playground became just a gray shadow scissored up by the Venetian blinds, where there were some monkey bars looking lonely and foreign in some snow, all through kindergarten.

Sometimes Mrs. Talifero brought a big box full of instruments out of her closet. These weren't instruments like violins or flutes, but blocks and sticks and things with handles that had sandpaper taped to them. There were a few tambourines—some of which were tiny and you played with just two fingers. And there was a drum—like an Indian's drum, with feathers on it. Eventually the stick with a big rubber ball on its end got broken. After that, Mrs. Talifero told the kindergartner who got that drum just to play it by hitting it with a fist.

And that was Richie's favorite.

The way his own fist could make a whole drum thump.

But kindergarten only lasted half a day. It ended when morning ended and another group of kindergartners took their places—their seats and instruments and their nappy mats—and Richie suspected that when their day was over these others also lined up at the door to say goodbye to Mrs. Talifero before they went out into the hallway to put their boots on again.

Strangers' boots.

The school was just around the corner from his house, so Richie could walk home by himself. Unlike his friends, who were picked up by their mothers, all he had to do was walk across the school's front yard, turn a corner, turn another corner (never needing to cross a street), and he was home, and his mother would be at the door, and his little brother would be in his highchair, and a grilled cheese sandwich would be waiting for him on the kitchen table with a glass of apple juice.

He'd been gone forever, but it was only lunchtime.

Richie watched his mother write JOLLY ROGERS on the envelope. He knew letters by then. He was learning them in kindergarten.

"Do you remember the pool, Richie? Do you want to go to it again this year? Because we need to go more this summer. The membership dues to the swim club are very expensive."

"Yes!" Richie said, unable to pretend any longer not to remember. "I *love* the pool!"

He might even have shouted it.

He put his arms around his mother's legs and squeezed them hard. She laughed and put her hand on his head, pulling softly at one of his curls, and said, "Okay, okay, I thought so. I just wanted to make sure before I put this check in the mail."

Yes!

He remembered . . .

Aqua blue. And how every time he got into that water, there was the shock of its cold, and how his heart seemed to stop before it started to beat harder. And he remembered trying to keep his feet on the bottom, but then he was floating, like he was an astronaut. Then gravity came back when he got out and his swim trunks sagged down, dripping water, and his mother would tie the string that held them up tighter.

And how the sun made an empty bowl out of the sky. And the reddish prickling of the sun's fire on his shoulders.

And the picnic basket, and the peanut butter sandwiches wrapped in waxed paper. Some grapes or apples. Some Oreos or chocolate chips. A thermos of lemonade or Tang. The little tin cup that came with the thermos and tasted like a brand new spoon. The smell of green when the grass around the pool had just been mown. The mothers behind the fence, on that soft grass, lying in their lounge chairs. Their flowered hats. Their big sunglasses. The smell of coconut from their lotions.

The pool had only been yesterday, it seemed to him, remembering, but it had also never happened!

9

The countdown had been followed by the liftoff—which seemed to take place in slow motion despite the ball of orange (for those who owned color TVs) exploding under the rocket as the scaffolding fell away, after which cheers could be heard being sent up from all the other houses on every block.

It was summer, so everyone's windows were open.

Two hours later, the Jolly Rogers Swim Club team won their first meet of the summer.

8

Although Becca had forgotten the name of that swim club until her professor said it, it all came back to her then in that darkened classroom. The sudden chemical sting of its water in her sinuses and tear ducts. Chlorine. That sweet poison. How the scent of it would stay in her hair long after it was washed.

Becca had felt fearless, weightless, immortal in that pool that summer. She wasn't technically allowed in the deep end since she was under twelve and hadn't passed the club's required tests or classes, but she swam in it anyway, lured by the otherworldly blue, which was so much brighter and more insistent—dazzling, dreamlike—than any color she'd ever seen with her own eyes in the real world before or since.

It could have been the best summer of her life—her new stepfather and his nice house, the nice car he'd bought Becca's mother, the new West Mission Hills neighborhood they'd moved into from the one Becca had not known was dangerous until she'd lived in a different kind of neighborhood. They'd eaten at restaurants sometimes three or four nights a week, and her stepfather bought them the swim club membership—happily writing a check for their dues, ripping it out of his checkbook with the sound of a fly being swatted before he handed it over to Becca's mother and said, "This'll give all of you some recreational fun for the summer."

But Becca's mother didn't like water. And Becca's new stepsister, Chrissy, was terrified of the pool and the children in it. Her new stepbrother, Davey, was too old to go to the pool. He had friends. His friends came to the house every day, disappearing with him into the basement.

But all of that was fine. Becca had her own membership card, which she could show to the girl who sat at the entrance to the tunnel between the parking lot and the pool. Becca's hand would be stamped, showing that she was a member. So she could swim all day. And she had a bike, so she could get to the pool by herself.

The bike!

Her stepfather had taken her to the store and told her to pick out any bike she wanted, although, at first, he'd objected to the bike she picked out.

"Sweetheart," he said. "That bike's too big for you. Even if I lower the seat, you're going to be stretching your legs as far as they'll go to pedal it. That's a bike for a teenager, not a little girl." He took her over to a little girl's bike—sparkly and purple with plastic streamers on its banana-handled bars, which Becca didn't like at all.

The only bike she liked was the one that was too big for her. It was the color of a robin's egg.

But she didn't say anything to her stepfather. Before they'd even opened the door to the bike shop she'd decided she would take whatever bike he would buy her. Until then, the only bike she'd ever ridden—the bike on which she'd been taught to ride—had belonged to the daughter of one of her mother's boyfriends, Phil. It, too, had been a kid's bike. Phil's daughter had moved to Maine with her mother, so Phil had said, even after he and Becca's mother broke up, that Becca could have it. But the day Phil came to pick up his shaving kit and his space heater, he took the bike, too. And Becca didn't want to have another bike like that one ever again, and the purple one her stepfather thought she might like better looked like that one.

"Oh, for goodness' sake!" her stepfather said when Becca nodded sadly at the bike he wanted to buy her. "Let's just get the other one if you love it so much!"

Then he tore another check from his whole book of them, and soon he was wheeling that blue bike to his car in the parking lot for her.

Becca stood to the side as her stepfather folded it into the back seat. He still seemed worried, though, and said, "I hope you can ride this bike, baby. I know you love it, but you might have to grow into it. You might not be able to ride this bike for a year! You aren't going to be able to put your bottom on the seat and reach the pedals!"

But Becca did not have to wait a year to ride the bike.

She could push the pedals without sitting down.

It wobbled, but also sailed, down the sidewalk.

She rode it so quickly that, sometimes, she passed the cars driving down the street beside her.

She loved the sound it made—a slick kissing noise as the tires rolled smoothly over cement, turning even the bumpy cracks into velvet.

And the white wicker basket between the handlebars!

That had been an "accessory." Meaning it didn't just come with the bike. This they were told at the register.

"So, do you want the basket, too?" Becca's stepfather had asked.

The man at the register cracked his knuckles behind the counter as he waited for Becca to answer.

But she couldn't.

She felt her throat fill up with something that tasted to her like tears, but tears that weren't coming out of her eyes. She was shedding tears, it seemed to her, from behind her face. How many times in her life had she been told, upon reaching a cash register, that what they were planning to buy they wouldn't be buying after all because it was more expensive than the price tag said it would be? Becca wanted the basket as much as she wanted the bike, but she didn't want to risk losing both, so she swallowed, looked down at her sneakers, and said no.

Her stepfather laughed and said to the man at the cash register, "Oh, we want the basket, too, I believe." Then he ripped up the check he'd already written and wrote another one, adding extra numbers for the basket. And then they were driving home with her new bike in the trunk. Then they were in the driveway, taking it out of the trunk. When Becca's mother saw it, she gasped and kissed Becca's stepfather, and then she looked down at Becca and said, "I hope you've been properly grateful for this expensive present."

It wasn't until then that Becca realized that she'd barely said a word to her stepfather the whole way home. She'd been too excited. And, while still at the bicycle shop, she hadn't dared to say anything, being fearful of sounding greedy. Also, she didn't really know her stepfather. Once, when he'd given her a ten-dollar bill to spend at the toy store, she'd thrown her arms around his neck, and he'd pushed her away. Gently, but she was embarrassed. She hadn't known, since he and her mother got married, whether she was supposed to hug him. Phil, her mother's boyfriend, had asked to be hugged every night. ("You're not going to bed without giving me a big hug!" he'd say.) So she'd hug him whether she wanted to or not. She hadn't liked how he smelled. Spicy, but not clean. She didn't know yet what her stepfather smelled like. They hadn't hugged.

So, at home, in front of her mother, Becca said, "Thank you for the bike. And for the basket."

"Oh, no!" her mother said. "Did you pay extra for a basket? She doesn't need a basket, too!"

Her stepfather laughed and said, "None of your business, my dear!" and kissed Becca's mother. "I've got some work to do now, but you go find a good place in the garage for your bike, Becca. In the corner? By the rakes?" He opened the front door of his house, waved goodbye, and stepped inside.

Becca put her hands on the handlebar grips then and was ready to flip the kickstand up with the toe of her sneakers when suddenly her neck was being bent backward and her face had been turned to the sky. Her ponytail was in one of her mother's hands, being pulled, hard. With her other hand her mother scratched the soft place under Becca's chin with her long fingernails, and then she whispered loudly into Becca's ear—the breath of it hot and smelling like ashes:

"*That's* how you say *thank you* to your father for a present like *this*?"

Becca struggled away from her mother. Her neck hurt. And the fingernails under her chin were digging in. Then, she stumbled and fell sideways, and the new bike fell, too.

"Look what you did!" her mother shouted.

Oh, no.

Becca knelt beside her bike.

There was a scrape in the blue paint. The wicker basket was dented. When she started to cry, her mother leaned over and slapped Becca in the mouth and said, "Don't you dare say a word about this to your father!"

"He's not my *father*!"

Becca put her hands over her own ears to keep her ear drums from being punctured by the shrill volume of her own scream. But her mother slapped her in the ear then, harder than her mouth, and Becca's whole head vibrated with it, but she stood up anyway and wheeled her bike to the garage. All that night, she could hear nothing out of her ear except for the sound of a tiny drum being thumped by a fist.

7

The night before he left for his business trip to Atlanta, and then to Dallas, Richard drew a diagram for his wife and son.

Alex looked on, but he was only interested in the pencil with which Richard sketched, trying to reach out of his highchair to grab it from his father's hand.

Richard had tried to get out of his meetings so he could be home to explain space flight and rocket engineering to Richie as they watched the launch together. It had taken him a week to get up the nerve to ask Barrett if someone else might take his place in Dallas. He'd asked nearly a month in advance, which was plenty of notice, and there were several salesmen without kids who could take the trip and who would enjoy it.

"Why? What's the problem?" Barrett asked.

Richard told his boss the truth. The launch. He wanted to be home to watch it with—

But Barrett cut him off before he could mention his son.

"Oh, so you're a space guy, Manning? Well, don't worry. They'll have TVs where you're going, Spaceman."

Richard cleared his throat. He said, "I know they will, Barrett. Of course, but my son is at an age—"

"Wait! I'm sorry, Richard! So your son's an astronaut already? Is he Buzz or is he Neil?"

Richard pretended to laugh. He said, "No, he's only five. So I'd like to watch it with him."

"Well," Barrett said. "What *I'd* like is for you to do the job you were hired to do. And I'd also like you to get out of my office. We *all* have work to do, Manning, since most of us aren't going to be going to the moon, even though we'll be paying for it with our taxes, so somebody around here needs to make some money. And that someone, Spaceman, would be you. Welcome to America, my friend."

Richard nodded and said, "Thank you for considering." Then he walked out of Barrett's office, closing the door carefully and quietly behind him.

What he'd wanted to do after that was to turn around and open the door again, stand in front of the fat bastard and tell him, "I quit. You can sell office furniture for the rest of your life, but *I'm* going to get a real job and make some real money."

Why didn't he?

Richard knew he was leaving the company eventually. His brother-in-law had told him there would be a place for him at AmeriWay whenever he was ready—"When you've got the balls, you've got the job!"—and *that's* where the real money was being made.

And Richard was ready to make it.

But Richard also had to imagine himself going home to tell Marie that he'd quit his job. Then he'd have to listen to her cry. She would be scared. His wife was scared of everything. She especially didn't like the idea of Richard following his sister's husband to AmeriWay. She wouldn't tell Richard why, would only say, "I don't understand it, Richard. They sell laundry detergent. You sell furniture. Furniture is more expensive, and it's more *real.* Todd can't possibly be making as much money as you are. Either that or it isn't *real* money. They have to be in debt, with that house and—"

"That house? That house is how we know how much money Todd makes!" Richard said. "They all have houses like that, Marie. Mansions! Do you think I can't do it? Is that what you're saying? Are you saying that you're scared that I'm not as—?"

"That's not what I'm saying! But we have a house that's just the right size for us. We don't need—"

"Need! Who *needs* to be rich, Marie? You have to *want* things in this life!"

"Well, I don't want anything we don't need!"

"Okay, well, we *need* a goddamn roof on this house is what we need, and we can't afford one!"

"We'll save money for that, Richard. We don't need the swim club. We don't—"

"Your problem, Marie, is that you don't know how to think big. You and the whole Pulaski gang. Nobody ever accused any of you of being ambitious, that's for sure! And where'd your dad go, huh? You think a man married to a ball buster like your mother was going to stick around?"

Marie said nothing, so Richard went on.

"Well, I wasn't raised like you, and my sister is nothing like you. The Mannings know how to think big. My sister knows how to stand by a husband who can buy her a real house. Not a house like this. A house like *theirs*!"

Marie started then, of course, to cry.

But his brother-in-law's was an incredible house—brick, with at least seven bedrooms and three bathrooms and a fountain in the backyard. How could Marie not want such a house if all Richard had to do was get another job to buy it? Hadn't she been the one fretting about the roof, the leak, how there was water dripping through the ceiling in the Richie's room, in the first place? And how exactly did she think they were going to pay for it? She'd suggested they drop the swim club membership, which was further proof to Richard of how little his wife understood about money. The swim club dues were no small expense, but the money they'd save dropping the membership wouldn't make a dent in the expense of a new roof. Richard needed twice the salary he made to pay for that, and he could make twice as much at AmeriWay, and then he could buy them not only a new roof but a mansion!

But even if he couldn't quit that day and face his wife that night, Richard, walking away from his boss's office, knew that he was done with that job, and that soon he would be moving on to an entirely new life, blasting off, taking his family with him.

6

Ants.

Marie turned her back to the phone on the wall and wiped the counter down with her cloth one last time as she watched one of the many ants that were making their house their home feel its way across the kitchen counter on its way to the sugar bowl.

It had a mission, and so did Marie. She tore a paper towel from the roll of them. She planned to snatch that ant up and, with her thumb and index finger and that paper towel, pop it like a horrible berry.

Before she did, she called over her shoulder, "Richie! We can go to the pool now!"

Silence.

The ant knew where it was going.

Richie had been in such a hurry.

Where was he now?

"Richie?"

The ant seemed to sense that Marie was there and to suspect what she planned to do. It began to move more quickly, still headed in the direction of the sugar bowl. She reached toward it with the paper towel before she thought—*No. Just leave it.*

What was the point?

It couldn't get into the bowl, which had a very tight seal, anyway. Eventually—probably after she and Richie and Alex were already on their way home from the pool that afternoon—that ant would realize the folly of its ambition and head for the crack under the kitchen door again, and then maybe it might even be able to find its way back outside.

Disappointed. But alive.

Marie put the paper towel on the counter and flipped the light switch and turned toward the living room to find her sons.

"Richie!"

They weren't in the living room.

The television had been turned off.

Richie must have gotten bored of Walter Concrete, as he called him.

The front door was open, and for a moment Marie thought—

But no.

Of course not.

Richie would never take Alex outdoors without asking for permission. Also, the screen door had a broken spring and it wheezed when it was opened and slammed closed, so she'd have heard them leave.

"Richie?"

Marie looked out the screen door, just in case. No one was out there to be seen except for a little girl riding a bicycle down the sidewalk across the street.

The bike was too big for her. She wobbled. She had to stand to press the pedals. A towel spilled out of a wicker basket between her handlebars. A long red comet tail of hair streamed behind her.

That girl couldn't have been more than a couple years older than Richie. One day, Marie realized, he would want to ride a bike, by himself, to the swim club, too—some summer afternoon in the future.

But not yet.

He still needed training wheels.

They had taught him about crosswalks and how to stop his bike when he got to the end of a corner, and he could do that, but Marie couldn't imagine a time when she would stay home while either of her little boys rode off alone on a bicycle.

That girl on her pale blue bike with its fat tires and with her long red hair flowing behind her came and went with nothing more than the sound of a thread being snipped with a sharp pair of scissors, and then Marie turned around and found Richie standing behind her, holding his brother's hand. Alex had his pacifier in his mouth and was blinking slowly up at her.

"Where have you been?" she asked him.

"Here," he said, and pointed to himself.

"Well, it's time to go," she told him. "Don't forget your towels and toys."

"You put them in the car already," Richie said.

She had?

Marie didn't remember that.

She closed and locked the front door before picking Alex up, heading through the kitchen to the back door.

Richie followed.

He didn't run.

Marie looked back at him and was surprised that he wasn't jumping up and down, at least.

Alex's diaper smelled soaked and warm, but she could change it in the locker room at the swim club.

She opened the back door to let Richie out, and then she glanced back toward the kitchen counter.

That ant had already reached the sugar bowl somehow. It had already begun to climb its ceramic side.

Marie hoisted Alex up to a more comfortable spot on her hip and stopped for a moment to watch.

Such a lot of effort, she thought, to reach the sugar bowl, only to find a rubber seal around the lid. Still, it might not be a complete waste of time and energy. There might be *some* bit of sweetness it could taste around that rim of the lid. Even after it became clear to the ant that there was no possibility of reaching the actual source of that sweetness, there might still be some pleasure to be taken in having gotten so close to it.

She closed the door.

5

"Well, I don't think it's necessarily pity we're feeling for you, Sarah. It's perhaps more like concern. And understanding," Steve said. "We've all been there, and we could all end up there again."

I didn't bother to pretend to consider this.

No one moved. No one even seemed to breathe or blink.

After a long enough pause had passed that I knew Steve wouldn't let it go on much longer, I said, "Thanks. But I think we should just move on. Let's hear from someone else now. It was a long night. I told you everything I can remember."

I alone laughed at my black-out joke.

"Why?"

It was Bethany.

I wasn't scared of Bethany.

"Why what?" I asked her.

We'd been friendly for a month or so when I first moved to Littleton and chose the meetings at Holy Redeemer, randomly, from a list of AA meetings on a sheet of paper tacked to the bulletin board by the bathrooms at the public library, but that had ended when she'd asked me if I was a Christian and I said, "Most definitely not." She didn't respond except to look at me like she knew something about me that I didn't know she knew, so I'd never sat next to her at any meetings since.

"Well, why should we move on to someone else?" Bethany asked, while looking, it seemed to me, at something far beyond my right shoulder. "Why do you prefer to listen to us than to talk to us?"

She was ten years younger than I was, which I knew because she'd told us months earlier that she was twenty-two, *and I've made the kind of mess of my life that it takes most people half a century to make.*

I said nothing.

There was nothing to do but stare at my scraped kneecap now that I had plucked all the stray threads over it away.

Bethany went on.

"We told you our stories, *Sarah.* Give us yours."

It was true that I'd said less about myself than others, and to be honest I'd felt stingy a few times after hearing about some son's Christmas morning spent with a raging hangover at the county jail instead of his parents', or the surprise visit to an alcoholic mother from Child Protective Services while she was asleep at noon on a Monday and the kids were playing outside in the snow in their pajamas instead of at school, but I certainly wasn't prepared to tell any stories that night, so I simply said, "I don't have anything more to say, Bethany, but I truly appreciate your concern."

Bethany sighed. Shook her head. Put two fingers to each of her temples and suddenly shouted, "Oh, *bullshit.* Come on. Tell us all about it! Why'd you show up here tonight if you didn't want *to tell us all about it*?"

"About *what*?" I shouted back at her.

Bethany mumbled something then and shook her head.

She was so incredibly young and fucked up, I thought.

I said, "Go to hell."

Steve stood up then, but that's all he did. The Big Book that had been on his lap fell on the floor and skidded until it was almost at the center of our circle.

But my words sounded less angry and defiant than I'd hoped they would. Watered down. And they'd kind of caught in my throat coming out of me, snagging somewhere behind my tonsils. Before our unspoken falling-out, after Bethany asked me if I was a Christian, I recalled that after one meeting she'd asked me if I would like to come over to her apartment for dinner some night. She could make pancakes and bacon. It would be breakfast for dinner. When I said thank you but no, Bethany just smiled and said the invitation would always be open if I changed my mind.

Had she hated me since then or since our talk about Jesus?

She continued to shake her head, and something about the resignation of it, the it's-not-worth-it-anyway of it, made me very angry.

"Did you hear me?" I asked her. "I said you can go to hell."

Bethany said, "Okay, I'll go to hell if that will make you happy. I know I belong in hell. But how about you? You're an alcoholic, too, obviously, but unlike the rest of us you don't have any problems with yourself? Well, in that case you can just tell us all what's so special about you? How have *you* managed to avoid—"

She didn't finish. She rolled her eyes at the ceiling's fluorescent light.

Had she hated me even before I rejected her invitation to breakfast or answered her question about Jesus sarcastically?

Clearly.

But, why?

Did she know me, or about me, from some other place and time?

Impossible.

The only person in New Hampshire who even knew my real name was Wolfie.

Still, I wanted to grab my purse and hurry out of the basement of Holy Redeemer, taking only enough time to tell them *all* to go to hell before I vanished from their lives forever.

But could I pull off a smooth exit like that with this hangover?

No.

I closed my eyes.

Steve nervously started to clear his throat.

4

It took forever to get to the pool. Even after they were finally out of the house and into the car, Richie's mother had to go back inside again. Alex had dropped his pacifier. The last time it was left at home, Alex had started to scream his word for pacifier, "Boppy! Boppy!" and sob until their mother bought him a popsicle—which hadn't seemed fair to Richie, who hadn't screamed at the pool and hadn't gotten a popsicle, and also because Alex didn't even know how to suck on a popsicle. Their mother had to hold it to his mouth and let him lick it until almost all of it had melted onto the grass.

But so much wasn't fair.

For instance, only Richie's little brother was allowed to eat in the car because of "the mess." But because his mother would hand a baggie of Fruit Loops to Alex when he started to fuss, there was a dust of colorful sugar all over the back seat.

"Why can't I—?"

Richie would start to ask about unfairness, but whenever he did his mother would tell him that it was because he was a big boy and Alex was a baby.

"You're a big boy, Richie. You need to act like a big boy."

And Richie *was* big.

That was true.

Richie was going to be in first grade soon, and Alex couldn't even use the potty yet.

And first grade was *real* school.

Richie knew this, having seen the first-grade classroom whenever he and the other kindergartners were walked down the hallway by their teacher to the gym or music room.

There was a window next to every classroom door, and through the first graders' window Richie could see the first graders—how they sat at desks, in rows, not at tables, in a circle. The first graders held real pencils, too—the kind that Richie wasn't allowed to use because he might poke out his eye—not crayons. And there were no carpet squares piled up in a corner for naptime. There was, it seemed, no nap time. Whenever they passed that classroom, Mrs. Talifero would turn, put a finger to her lips, and say, "*Shhhh.* We have to be quiet. The students are learning."

They would be so quiet that no first graders ever even looked up from those desks.

That's how quietly the kindergarteners were walking and how hard the first graders were learning.

Everything was as quiet as nothing.

Learning required this.

The way everything else required *patience.*

Whenever Richie's mother used that word he could feel the weight of it settle in the bottom of his stomach. That word felt the way it would feel if you ate the kind of paste for which you needed a popsicle stick to dig it out of a jar when things needed to be stuck to other things—hearts, stars, alphabet letters. Tommy Smith ate a lot of paste with his stick once when Mrs. Talifero wasn't looking, but Richie had no interest in eating paste. He thought it would lump up inside your stomach where you couldn't see it. And this, to him, was like *patience*—trying to have it in the back seat next to your baby brother while your mother stopped at every red sign on the way to the pool.

The world of grown-ups moved so slowly.

Even the spaceship had taken forever to blast off that morning.

First, they'd counted down: *10, 9, 8.*

Then, they paused: *7, 6, 5.*

Another pause. *4, 3, 2.*

And then a pause that went on forever:

1.

But even after that, nothing very fast happened.

Some fire came out of the rocket, but the rocket didn't *blast.* It was a slow rocket. It was so slow that Richie understood that it would take a very long time to get to the moon. So even astronauts had to be patient.

"Stop it," his mother said.

"Stop what?" Richie asked.

"You know what," his mother said.

But Richie did not know what. So, he didn't stop.

"I told you to stop kicking the seat!" his mother said.

Oh.

Richie stopped that.

He looked out the window and saw a girl riding a beautiful blue bicycle down the sidewalk. She had a white wicker basket between the handlebars of her bike, and a towel was stuffed into the basket. She wore a purple bathing suit and had very long red hair that floated in the air behind her as she rode her bike. Standing up on her bike, leaning down on her handlebars, she was hunched over, concentrating. It was a really big bike. It was a lot slower than a car. By the time that red-haired girl got to Jolly Rogers on that bike, Richie would already have been in the pool *forever.*

Still, he envied the girl.

She had a grown-up's bike.

She could go to the pool by herself, riding that bike whenever she wanted to go—*wherever* she wanted to go—as soon as she was ready.

Then his mother stopped at another sign, and the little girl caught up to their car, and then she turned the corner and was ahead of them.

She would be at the pool *before* them!

All these stop signs!

They would *never* get to the pool.

"Richie, I said *stop that,*" his mother said. And this time he knew what she meant so he stopped, but he crossed his arms and stared at his feet and knew that he would be a man like his father by the time they finally got even to the parking lot of the pool. He'd know how to mow a lawn and how to make a knot at his neck with a tie before they got out of the car. By the time they got the picnic basket out of the trunk and his mother had Alex on her hip, Richie would be sitting at a desk, holding a pencil for his whole life, like a first grader. Before they ever got to the entrance of the tunnel—that long damp darkness that smelled like his grandmother's cellar between the parking lot and the pool he'd already be a very old man! With a cane! He'd already have married a grown-up lady. He might already be a boy who puts groceries into bags at the end of a counter. He would definitely already have gone on the vacation they were going to take *next summer.* Yellowstone Park, where there was a volcano that blasted water into the sky according to schedule every day, an idea he liked, not having to ask anybody how long until something happened because you knew when that water would blast.

Old—

Something.

His father had told him about it. When his father was a little boy and his own father was a father and alive, he saw it. This was before Richie's father's father became a grandfather and couldn't breathe without a tube and then got put in a box in the ground where he was going to be kept forever.

Richie never saw that box. He just heard about it from his cousin Stacy, who babysat Richie and Alex during the funeral instead of going to it.

"Why didn't you go to Grandpa's funeral?" Richie asked, hoping she'd say that it was because she wanted to play Chutes & Ladders with him, but she said, "Because I don't need to see the fucking funeral. See Grandpa in a box." She shook her head at the idea of it.

Stacy hadn't wanted to play games that day either. That day she just wanted him to play by himself in the living room while she sat in the kitchen and held a bottle to Alex's mouth, holding the phone in her other hand.

His parents were at the funeral forever. When they got home, wearing black clothes and seeming unhappy, Richie looked up from the Chutes & Ladders game he was trying to play by himself and asked them if the fucking funeral was already over, and they didn't answer him.

"If you don't stop it, Richie, *right now,* I'm going to turn this car around and we'll go straight home."

He kicked the seat one more time, but very softly so she couldn't feel it, and then he saw the sign:

JOLLY ROGERS SWIM CLUB.

And then he was happy, and then time sped up so fast that his mother was already putting her car keys in her purse. And then, suddenly, Richie was carrying the picnic basket for her "like a big boy" and walking beside her across the parking lot toward the entrance, which was the tunnel, toward the girl with two long black braids who had been there for a long time, waiting for them. She looked at their membership cards and found their names on her list and stamped the backs of their hands with the red letter, J, which meant that they were members of the club.

After the stamp the girl said, "Have fun," and she flipped one of her black braids over her shoulder and turned to say hello to someone standing behind Richie's mother. Someone who was also waiting for the stamp.

It was the red-haired girl!

She was holding in her arms the towel he'd seen in the wicker basket between her bike's handlebars a million minutes ago.

How?!

How had she gotten to the pool *so fast*?

She'd been *so far* behind them!

She'd been too small for her big bike!

"Stop staring at me," the red-haired girl said in a loud whisper.

Richie stopped staring.

His mother took his hand.

Then, he was inside the tunnel.

He forgot about the girl.

He saw a flash of light, and then he saw two different kinds of blue and the back of the white chair in which the lifeguard sat between them.

3

Richard Manning wanted his son's casket to be made of mahogany, with 24-carat gold hinges, and he didn't care what it cost.

However, the faceless and hairless man who took Richard and Marie into the basement of the funeral home to show them their options told Richard that, although not impossible, in his many years at the funeral home, there'd never before been ordered a custom-made casket. It would take some time, surely—not only for something like that to be made, but to find a craftsman to make it, and to commission the work to Richard's specifications, and, well, *the expense.*

"I'm just guessing at this," the man said. "But the expense. Mr. Manning, it would be extraordinary, at least ten, maybe a hundred times the price of any of the caskets you see here."

That's when Marie squeezed Richard's elbow and said, "He's right."

The funeral director's assistant—or whatever he was: a salesman moonlighting from the used car lot, or the embalmer moonlighting in the casket room, or the family idiot employed out of necessity by the Metzger Family Funeral Home?—was inspired, hearing Marie. He went on:

"Also, of course, the most unfortunate thing of all would be that the funeral service would need to be put off for an unusually long time. Really, I have no idea how long the crafting of such a coffin might take. In a situation like this, we always advise that the funeral service take place within a few days of the—"

"Drowning," Richard said.

"Yes. Everyone needs to come together as soon as possible. For your boy. For themselves. I suggest no later than Sunday, but we couldn't possibly plan the service if we're going to commission a custom-made—"

"Casket," Richard said.

"Please, Richard," Marie said.

He shook her grip off his arm and said, "I don't care about the cost. Someone out there can make it. The service can wait. My son will spend the rest of his life in that—"

Marie put her hands over her face and ran toward the stairs leading out of the basement. He and the casket salesman could both hear her sobs trailing after her long after she had left the showroom. Neither man spoke again for several minutes. Then, the idiot member of the Metzger Family Funeral family cleared his throat and said, "To wait would mean, of course, that an open casket service would likely no longer be a possibility."

He didn't tell Richard why.

He didn't have to.

"And, sir, I believe that Mrs. Manning is quite set on the service being held by Sunday, and perhaps that change of plans, and waiting longer, could cause her even greater pain?"

"Just shut up then," Richard said. "Just shut up."

And so it was that Richard Manning let himself be talked into burying his son in a mass-market casket that he chose from one the prototypes displayed in the basement of the local funeral home while his wife wailed in the ladies' room above him.

2

Many of the pictures taken that day, after they were returned to those who'd snapped them from the photo shop or pharmacy developer, captured none of the swimmers and their smiles. The day had been too bright for details. Shared with neighbors or others who'd been there before the boy drowned, there was some talk of omens. Surely some sign was to be found in all that annihilating light. And some saw, in the vague outline of the trophy that managed to bleed gold into a few of the prints, not a miniature swimmer made of brass about to dive from a board but an angel holding the body of a child in her arms.

Omens, too late, were everywhere, afterward.

But a few of the cameras aimed at the swim team managed to capture not only the swim team and their trophy, but the lifeguard behind them, and some of these would be printed on the front page of the newspaper.

She wore her sunglasses, held a paper cup. She sipped from a straw stuck into its lid. She wore white shorts with her swimsuit. Her hair was blond and straight. Her legs were tan. She looked like a starlet playing the part of a lifeguard in a foreign film about young Americans, cast by a director fond of both teenage girls and stereotypes.

Dan Applegate had been standing beside the snack bar when the photos were taken, so he appeared in none of them, but he'd watched them being taken and said, "Hey," to the lifeguard after her posing was done and the swim team members had wandered off to the locker rooms. "How's it going?"

"It's gone!" the lifeguard said.

It was a joke he'd made himself in June, which she'd repeated to him ever since.

She was wearing a small silver cross on a silver chain around her neck and little silver doves in her pierced ears. She smelled like strawberries.

In another year, Dan would send a letter to her from Vietnam, to which she would never respond. He would hope she never got his letter, or that hers had been lost at battalion headquarters.

But he would never know.

1

The lifeguard's mother went to the kitchen after closing the front door. She stood in front of the sink, trying to remember what it was she'd meant to do. It was in the middle-depth of her memory, trying to swim to the surface where she could consider it—something to do with housework?

Something not urgent but also not forgettable?

She almost remembered before it slipped back into a place in her skull she couldn't reach.

She rubbed her forehead.

Goodness.

She'd meant to do something!

But by the time she would remember what it was, the Manning boy would already have been buried for several days under a pink granite stone at the Mission Hills Cemetery, and the house would be buzzing and swarmed with flies.

Because what she'd meant to do was to find the flypaper (which Bob had kept in the cellar with the other dangerous things, and which had stayed there, untouched, since he died) and to set it out, but the lifeguard's mother's memory could only reach as far as the sense of some sticky rosin and the smell of something poisonously sweet.

In the meantime, the flies were laying eggs, and the eggs would soon be hatching, and a new booming generation of houseflies would find their way into the attic through a crack in the roof, attracted by the darkness and the proximity of humans—the flesh and food those flies could sense beyond the old baby clothes and photo albums.

Most of them would never make it out of the attic. They'd just buzz around in that dark brain of the little house and mummify on top of boxes labeled WEDDING FLOWERS and BAPTISMAL

GOWN and drop into the pink insulation that frothed between the attic's floorboards.

But many others would find their way together to the kitchen, soon.

Three

1

No one noticed that there was no rope strung between the deep end and the shallow end of pool that afternoon. Or, if anyone noticed, no one thought to mention it to the swim coach, the lifeguard, or the snack bar boy, or to anyone else whose job it might have been to replace the rope, which stayed coiled beside the chain-link fence separating the pool from the grassy square where mothers read magazines under umbrellas.

Some of those mothers wore big sunglasses (like Jackie's) and some of them wore floppy straw hats with sunflowers glued to them. Mostly their bathing suits were modest, one-piece. But there were also some teenage babysitters in that area wearing bikinis, lying on towels in the grass, their bodies oiled, or sitting in a circle together playing card games, chewing gum or their fingernails or the tips of their long hair or sipping from straws stuck into soda cans.

Someone's transistor radio crackled out the familiar fuzz of a popular song.

The sky above them, into which those three handsome astronauts had disappeared hours earlier, was completely clear, empty of anything visible except for, now and then, a jet traveling across it—just a brief glimpse of a silver crucifix, dragging no white tail behind it, moving from one end of the pale blue sky to the other.

If that plane's pilot or passengers happened to look out of their windows, they'd have seen nothing but a small rectangle of aquamarine, which was the Olympic-sized pool in which Richie Manning drowned that afternoon between the deep end and the shallow end, where no rope had been strung after the swim meet that morning.

A beach ball twirled above the head of the seventy-two frothing, screaming children while the lifeguard sat above them, her bare feet hanging down over a white circle painted with a red cross and the stenciled word: *Lifeguard.*

She looked down, eyes hidden behind her polarized sunglasses, tan legs dangling from her throne, twirling her silver whistle between her index and middle fingers from the end of its lanyard, back and forth, while watching the flashing feet of the swimmers in their brightly colored bathing suits below her, but without ever noticing the boy, Richie Manning, as he drowned in the middle of the pool, where, usually, a rope was strung between the deep end and the shallow end.

2

Richard rode the escalator to his plane's departure gate at the Atlantic Municipal Airport. It was July 16, 1969. Everyone who was alive that day believed they would always remember where they were the morning the rocket launched those men to the moon to take the first human steps ever taken on its surface.

Richard made his way toward the Business Lounge, where there would be a television, around which, in a few minutes (if all went according to plan), those who were waiting in the airport in Atlanta for a connection to somewhere else could gather to watch.

He had wanted to watch the launch with his sons—or with Richie, since Alex was far too young to understand.

But Barrett had said, "There will be plenty more rockets, Richard. The moon isn't going anywhere. But we've only got one shot at Dallas. And your kids won't remember the moon anyway."

Barrett, however, was wrong.

Richie would remember.

Richie would never forget.

Richie was old enough that, one day, he would be able to tell his own children about how he'd been on Earth, in front of the television in their living room (since Marie had promised she'd remember to have Richie there) when everything changed.

Everything.

Richard couldn't help but think of his own father—dead for a year—and what this would have meant to him.

His father was a man who used to read—in a Scottish accent that he refused to lose, despite having left Scotland with his parents and their parents and all their extended relations for Canada (before Michigan) when he was younger than Richie was now—to Richard and his sister from a book he kept on the coffee table:

The American Epic.

The book had been about opportunity, about dreams, and Richard imagined that the book had offered some comfort to his father in exchange for the loss of the country his parents and grandparents had never stopped grieving.

Frequently his father's voice would catch in his throat (in a way that both moved and embarrassed Richard) when he read aloud that book's description of the US as *a land in which life should be better and richer and fuller for everyone, with opportunity for each according to his ability and achievement.*

And now Americans, who ruled the world, were conquering the moon, too.

Who knew what the future would be like when Richie and Alex were grown men? What opportunities might his sons have?

A woman two escalator steps above Richard was wearing a pantsuit—slick and white—with a patent leather purse (also slick and white) balanced on her hip.

The purse looked heavy, resting on that slender but sturdy skeletal bone. She twisted her hips in order to better bear the weight in such a way that the polyester of her pantsuit was stretched even more tightly than it had been. Richard could see the outline of her panties, which were white, like her pants, and he imagined that those panties were also silky, with a patch of soft cotton sewn into the crotch. Marie owned panties like that.

He looked away from the backside of that woman after thinking about Marie, and he glanced over the railing, where, below the escalator, he saw a mother wrestling with a little girl who seemed to be demanding to be carried onto the escalator, although the girl was at least six or seven years old.

The mother looked frail to Richard. That mother couldn't possibly carry the dead howling weight of her daughter on the escalator.

What was she doing alone with a child at an airport?

Where could she be going, alone, with a child?

When she tried to take her daughter's hand to guide her toward the escalator, the girl lay down flat on her back and slammed the heels of what appeared to Richard to be brand new shoes (pink, dressy) against the floor while a rivulet of businessmen passed around the drama, pretending not to notice it.

Richard wished he was still down there. He could have tried to help. He would have bent down and said to the girl, "What's the problem here, little lady?" And perhaps a strange man appearing above her might've provided enough surprise and distraction to get that girl on her feet and urged toward the escalator.

Where was the girl's father?

If Richard was still down there and not halfway up the escalator, he could've stepped in for that missing man, but it was too late now. The rocket launch was less than twenty minutes away, and Richard was going to be in the lounge, in front of that television, to watch, no matter what.

The woman in the white pants ahead of him hefted the burden

of her purse up and over her shoulder and began to click off in the direction of the Business Lounge, too, in her white high heels. Richard had no choice but to follow her, and his eyes wanted to watch her lead the way, but when an elderly couple passed him, he glanced away from the outline of that woman's panties to see the expression of disapproval on the shriveled face of the wife, who might even have glanced at Richard's hand, noting the gold band.

But Richard did not feel guilty about taking a lingering look at the back end of a woman wearing pants so tight that she was obviously inviting such lingering attention, but he didn't want to appear to others to be *that* kind of traveling salesman. Richard wasn't dead, so of course he saw women, everywhere, but he was a family man first. In his briefcase he had presents: a scarf for Marie, a plastic ax for Alex, and a yo-yo for Richie—a Deluxe Edition Duncan. It was a deep ruby red. It was so red that it was almost black. It would be his son's first yo-yo.

Also, Richard had only so recently gotten off the phone with Marie that it almost felt as if she was there with him, watching him suspiciously through the eyes of that old woman. His wife's voice had sounded, despite the payphone and the long distance, so clear and close that it was as if she had been speaking, physically, into his ear:

Where are you? Where will you be next? When will you be home? I know, I know, you already told me, Richard, but can you tell me again?

Richard told her again.

He was now headed from Atlanta to Dallas for one night, after which he'd have a brief stop in Cincinnati for lunch with the manager of a company with which his own company wished to do business. After that, he'd rent a car (using his travel expense account) and by Friday night, no later than 10:00 p.m., he would be home.

He reminded Marie that his secretary had typed up his itinerary and a carbon copy of it was on top of their dresser in the bedroom.

"Oh, that's right," Marie said.

In his imagination, Richard could see his wife staring out the window over the kitchen sink, having stretched the coiled cord of their wall-mounted phone as far as it would go. And whatever she saw out there displeased her—the grass getting longer, the fence between their property and the neighbors' rusting, the garage paint peeling, leaving a snow of white paint chips on the petals of the geraniums that she'd planted under the eaves.

Maybe these unmet chores of his felt like a betrayal to Marie—although she always said she understood that Richard worked too hard to maintain the house the way the retired husbands, and the unambitious ones, on their block took care of theirs. When he asked her if she'd rather be married to a man like Reg Waters across the street, who was always going to be a wage slave at that gear shaft manufacturing place but had plenty of time to push a lawn mower around and pull weeds on the weekends, Marie shook her head.

But Richard had no way of knowing what she really thought.

However, one day soon he would move her into a much (much) nicer house.

And if that house wouldn't make Marie happier, nothing would.

Which worried him—that nothing, in the end, would ever make Marie happy.

She took no pleasure whatsoever, it seemed to him, in the future. She was too concerned about the price of bread, and the ants—which no amount of poison seemed able to kill—to imagine the life they'd have in the house he was on his way to buying for them.

She just wanted to know when he'd be home.

And he'd already told her a hundred times.

No later than midnight tomorrow night.

Or, yes, 10:00 p.m. He'd said 10:00 p.m. . . .

"Don't forget to have Richie in front of the TV in half an hour," Richard said into the mouthpiece of the payphone's receiver, while, behind him, men like him hurried past with their briefcases swinging.

"Don't worry. We'll be watching."

"Can I talk to Richie?"

"Here he is. See you soon, Richard. Be careful. Call me from Dallas."

"Hi," he heard his son say, then, "Daddy?"

"Yes indeed!" Richard said. "This is Daddy. Is this Richie?"

"Yes," Richie said. "Hi, Daddy."

"Are you getting excited yet?"

"Yes," Richie said, but Richard had the feeling his son didn't remember what he was getting excited for.

"To the moon!" Richard said.

"Oh, right!" Richie said. "That's today!"

"Not long now! Be sure you're watching, okay? I'll be watching, too."

"Okay," Richie said.

"It's going to be a big blast, and fire, and everyone in the whole world will be watching."

"I know," Richie said. A pause. "And, Daddy, after that, guess what happens?"

"I can't guess. What happens after that, Richie?"

"After the moon, we're going to the pool!"

3

The first time Becca Brummler wheeled her bike out of the garage to ride it down the driveway, her stepbrother, seeing her from the front steps, laughed and said, "Oh my God. You look like an ant on that. You look like an ant trying to fly a jumbo jet."

It made Becca flush and, afterward, each time she rode it, she thought of herself as an ant.

But Becca was larger than an ant, and the bike was smaller than a jet. And although she could not, as her stepfather had warned her, reach the pedals and sit down at the same time, she could pedal standing up, and the bike would fly, and she would fly with it.

"You're a brat ant," her stepbrother said.

Seven days after her stepfather bought it for her, Becca went to the garage. She'd been told she needed to practice riding her bike every day for a week before she could have permission to ride it to the pool. This was the eighth day.

Becca stuffed her towel into the basket, getting ready. Her stepfather had sanded the spot that had scraped when the bike hit the driveway, and she had, herself, undented the basket. The bike was as good as new, but as soon as she hit the kickstand with the toe of her sneaker, Becca could tell that something was wrong.

She bent down to look.

The tires were completely flat. No air in them at all. The rubber sagged around the rims, which were the only thing between the bike and the cement floor of the garage.

Becca must have made a sound of despair and surprise—perhaps a loud cry—because her stepfather came out of the house to the garage then and asked her what was wrong.

She couldn't answer.

He knelt down next to the bike, fiddled around with the little nippled caps on the tires, and stood up again. His face was very red. He stepped out of the garage and shouted up at the open window of the attic, which Becca's stepbrother had made into a bedroom after she and her mother had moved in, and shouted, "David. DAVID! Get your ass down here right now."

Davey's face appeared at the small window then, taking all of that empty space up, looking gray behind the screen. His dirty-blond hair was messy. After the rocket launch that morning, he'd yawned and gone back to bed. He had just woken up again, it seemed.

"Now! Down here NOW!"

Davey disappeared.

Becca stood beside her bike while her stepfather stomped down to the end of the driveway and back. The screen door slammed, and Davey came out wearing the kind of silky shorts that runners wore. Neon green. He also wore a shark's tooth hanging from a strip of leather around his neck, and it dangled at the center of his chest, on which he had golden hairs that were spread out without any pattern—a tuft here, a few lonely filaments there. They sparked in the sun.

"What's up?" he asked his father.

"You know perfectly well what's up."

"No, I don't," Davey said.

"I told you to pump up Becca's tires last night. And you just unscrewed the caps and let the air out. I'm *assuming* you didn't do that on purpose, but if it happens again, I'll assume you *did*. Now go pump them up. She's going to the pool."

Davey shrugged and headed for the garage. He yawned as he passed Becca, but he managed to bump her in the chest with his elbow and when she put her hands over the pain he pulled her ponytail—one sharp tug that stung—without his father noticing.

4

He'd planned, later that day, when her shift was over and he was done behind the snack bar, as they walked out to the parking lot together (which they'd done together almost every day since the summer started) to ask the lifeguard if she'd like to go to a movie with him Friday night.

She'd told him once, through the snack bar window's screen during her break (Adult Swim), that she'd seen *2001: A Space Odyssey* and liked it, although she didn't understand it. So Danny Applegate had been studying the newspaper every night that week to see what was playing at The Escapade that was at all similar to *2001.*

Maybe *Marooned*?

That morning, Dan's father looked over his shoulder as he studied the movie listings at the kitchen table and asked if he was turning into a movie buff. "Or you planning a big date?"

Dan ignored him.

"Well, if you're going to bother asking some chick out on a date, son, and paying the big bucks for popcorn and all that, I vote that you ask that lifeguard out."

Dan's father had seen her, a few weeks earlier, while dropping Dan off at the swim club when his Chrysler wouldn't start and he needed to take Dan's car to work.

"Whooo-heeee," his father had said when the lifeguard got out of her own car and waved at Dan in his father's. "Get a load of that."

"She's the lifeguard, Dad," Dan told him.

"In that case, I'm drowning! Help!" his father said.

Dan tried not to laugh (it just encouraged him), but his father was so ridiculous it was hard not to.

"Ask her out, Danny Boy!" his father had said, clapping Dan's shoulder the way a father in a TV show might. "Bring her over to the house afterward! I'll show her my *Playboy* collection! She's got a career ahead of her!"

"Dad, *please*."

"Why not?"

"She might have a boyfriend or something," Dan said to his father.

But, despite himself, Dan lingered in the passenger seat beside his father, watching her.

He wanted, he realized, some advice from his father, who seemed to be considering the unfortunate possibility of a boyfriend seriously.

"Well, son," he finally said. "That never stopped me from asking a girl out! Your mother was married to my grandfather when I met her!"

Dan's mother was a few years older than his father, and the joke about her having been his step-grandmother was a constant.

"Come on, Dad. I don't want to mess this up. She's nice. I'm serious."

And Dan was serious. He didn't want to mess up. She was nice. As well as beautiful. She *must* have a boyfriend.

She and Dan didn't go to the same high school, so he had no idea what the lifeguard's life was like when she wasn't twirling her silver whistle around on its lanyard or walking with him out to the parking lot. It seemed unlikely that she wasn't dating the West Mission Hills High School quarterback or some older guy, already in medical school or the Army.

"Well, ask if she's got a boyfriend if you want to know!" his father said.

"Yeah, Dad. That'll be a smooth move. I'll just walk up to her and say, 'Do you have a boyfriend?'"

"No, Dumbo. Get a friend to ask her."

And, actually, that wasn't bad advice. Danny was glad he'd lingered for it. And later that day, he would take it. He'd asked his buddy who cleaned the pool to ask his sister, who went to West Mission High, if the lifeguard had a boyfriend. And it was reported back before the swim meet was even over that, no, in fact, she did not.

Dan's father shook his head slowly, watching as the lifeguard disappeared into the tunnel, and whistled wistfully, quietly. "I'm telling you, son, I've seen some sweet tail in my day, but that tail's so sweet I want to stick it in my mouth."

"Jeez, Dad."

Dan didn't get out of the car until the lifeguard was just a shadow cast on the entrance of the tunnel.

"Come on," his father said. "You gonna do this for us, son? You gonna be a man and ask little Miss America there to go to a porno with you tonight?"

"Dad!"

Dan instinctively looked over his shoulder

"Don't worry. Your mom's not in the back seat. She can't hear me."

To prove it, his father farted loudly.

"Come on. Please. Have mercy," Dan said as the same smell his father left behind him in the bathroom every morning filled the car.

His father laughed and said, "You didn't answer my question. Are you going to ask her out, son?"

"Yeah," Dan said.

Yeah, Dan thought.

And saying it out loud while also thinking it filled him with confidence and terror about the future.

5

There were, of course, those who would forgive anyone, for anything . . . *as He forgives those who trespass against us.*

It was easy for *them*, the others said, since it hadn't been *their* child who'd drowned at the Jolly Rogers Swim Club that day, had it?

Those who forgave the lifeguard didn't have anything to forgive her for, did they?

She might as well have killed that boy herself.

Someone from the Department of Motor Vehicles told his brother-in-law, who was the sports editor for the local paper, who reported it to the editor of the *Mission Hills Herald,* that the lifeguard had failed her first driver's license test because she'd run over an orange cone while attempting to parallel park. And her history teacher from Mission Hills High told friends and neighbors that the lifeguard had lost her expensive textbook the year before, having left it on a bench while showering after Phys Ed in the girl's locker room, where someone (someone who'd most likely lost her own textbook) had snapped it up, so the lifeguard's mother (very recently widowed) had been forced to pay for a replacement.

That inattentiveness, as well as her beauty—all that blond hair and those long legs and the big blue (or were they brown?) eyes behind her sunglasses—had drowned a kindergartner.

But she could have been paying attention!

Her lip gloss was evidence for this. Despite the chaos of the day, she'd managed to apply it, hadn't she?—strawberry flavored, it seemed, since those who had attempted to resuscitate the boy, after the lifeguard had failed to do so, told the media that there'd been the scent of strawberries on him.

And her toenails had been painted seashell pink. So she'd attended to *those* details, but she couldn't attend to the little detail of a boy drowning in the middle of the pool right in front of her pretty face? Had she forgotten that the reason she was sitting in that chair showing off her legs was to guard the lives of the children who had been entrusted to her?

Well, unless that lifeguard managed to figure out in a hurry how to raise the dead, she could never—ever—be forgiven.

6

The lifeguard unrolled the windows of her mother's Duster, the interior of which always smelled like winter, even in summer—the air seeming to be filtered through the heater's vents, bringing with it the sooty smell of January and February's engine fumes and stale air.

It was going to be a hot day. The lifeguard could feel the heat creeping down the street, following her, and rolling itself out ahead of her, too, so that the car's tires were beginning to attach themselves to the tar as they spun, pulling away with the sound of brief and showy kisses.

She knew that by the time she'd leave the swim club that afternoon, the car would be ovenlike, even if she left the windows unrolled. Even if she managed to slip into the one shady parking place in the Jolly Rogers Swim Club lot—near the entrance to the tunnel, under a leafy oak—by the time she got back out to it again the vinyl seat would be so stinging hot that she'd have to sit on her towel and she'd have to steer with her fingertips or burn her palms.

It was going to be a very, very busy day at the pool. Not only was there the heat, but this was the middle of the summer, the middle of summer vacation, the week of the season when almost all the members' families would either be home from any vacations they'd taken or would not yet have taken their vacations. And some parents might have rearranged their schedules to be sure to be home from Mackinac Island or from their cousins' cottages early enough to be in their own living rooms, in front of their own dependable television sets, to watch the rocket launch, to witness their children witness the beginning of a new era in human history—the most important event they would likely ever witness in their lives, the one they would never forget.

But the launch was over, so the midsummer boredom would already be back, worse than before. What seemed like years of excitement preceding the liftoff ended at *3, 2, 1!* Followed by scaffolding and fire. Then, just Walter Cronkite.

And even if the whole thing had cast a dreamlike glow over the day, those three astronauts were now just *in-between*, neither here nor there. There wasn't much more to be said on the television, so the children would want to go swimming.

There would be *so many children.*

Near the corner of Breton Avenue and Hall Street, the lifeguard slowed down as a fat white cat began a leisurely trek into the street, sauntering straight in front of the Duster.

The lifeguard waited and watched.

The cat didn't even glance up.

It just kept walking.

When she finally saw that the cat was safely on the other side of the street, climbing toward a skinny sapling in someone's front yard, the lifeguard took her foot off the brake. "Be more careful!" she called out the window. "Look both ways!"

The cat ignored her.

The lifeguard wondered whether or not it might be good omen to have a white cat saunter across the road in front of you. Maybe she should make a wish.

She laughed at the absurdity of this, but then she made a wish—

A wish that Danny Applegate would ask her to come over to his house that weekend and give her the musical education he kept teasing her she lacked.

She imagined drinking orange pop in some room of the house she imagined he lived in—a den. A poster of a famous guitar player she'd never heard of would be tacked to the wall above a small plaid couch. A record player would be on a shelf made of milk crates filled with albums. Danny would take out one of those albums, pull out the black vinyl inside it and blow the dust off it before he settled the record carefully onto the spinning turntable. Then he would very gently lower a very fine needle that would hover for what would seem like forever over that record before the music he wanted her to hear began to play.

7

Marie hoped that Richard hadn't been too wounded or disappointed by Richie's lack of enthusiasm about the rocket launch over the phone. Hopefully Richard understood that it wasn't that Richie wasn't excited to talk to his father, or about the rocket launch, but that their son simply did not yet understand the telephone, how no one could see him smile into it, that he was invisible to the person on the other end. Even if you could hear the other person. Even if the other person could feel your presence.

Last Christmas morning, while Richie was on the phone with Richard's sister, Marie had finally taken the phone receiver out of his hand. Pam had called to ask if Richie had liked the sled she'd dropped off a few days earlier. Marie knew her sister-in-law was on the other end of the line waiting for Richie to say he loved the sled (a red plastic thing, with a rope, which scared Marie, who imagined broken limbs, or worse) which had been so beautifully wrapped in gold paper that Marie wondered if Pam had paid someone to do it.

Richie had, of course, loved the sled. He held the phone receiver and jumped up and down excitedly. But he *said* nothing. So finally Marie took the phone and said, "Richie *loves* the sled, Pam. He screamed when he opened it. It's his favorite present, by far, and he's begging Richard to take him out on it right now. Unfortunately, he doesn't know that you can't see him smiling and nodding and jumping up and down."

Pam laughed and said she understood, but Marie wondered if she actually *did* understand, or if she thought poorly of Marie and Richard's parenting. Pam and Todd's children were ten years older than Richie and Alex. And, anyway, Pam and Todd's children seemed to have been *born* older. As toddlers they'd already known to say please and thank you and to put a napkin on their laps when they sat at a table.

After Richie stopped talking, Marie assumed Richard had said goodbye and hung up, but she took the phone from her son and said, "Richard? Are you still there?" in case he hadn't.

Nothing.

She was about to hang up, too, when she heard what sounded to her like breathing.

"Richard? Are you still there?"

A man laughed into her ear then.

It was not Richard's laugh.

This laughter was hoarse—loud, deep, false.

Marie gasped at the surprise and hung up. The bell inside the phone tried to ring but was aborted, stifled, still hidden somewhere beyond that harvest gold plastic. She turned away from it. She was trembling, she realized. She held her elbows in her hands so Richie couldn't see the trembling and asked him, "Richie, did you talk to anyone except Daddy on the telephone?"

"Nope," Richie said. He went back into the living room then, where Marie had already turned the television on, but nothing was happening yet. She followed him to it.

Richie got on the floor and took a plastic ambulance out of his brother's hand and began rushing it on its rubbery wheels across the carpet in the direction of a coffee table leg, beside which a matchbox racecar was flipped onto its roof after, presumably, smashing into the leg.

"Did you say goodbye to Daddy?" Marie asked him.

"Ummm, not really," Richie said. "Daddy did though."

So, the laughter had nothing to do with her husband, who'd already hung up. Lines had gotten crossed between the kitchen and Atlanta. It happened. Once, while talking to her mother on the phone, both of them began to hear another conversation going on under theirs. Two women were complaining about a neighborhood dog that wouldn't stop barking. And how they were going to take care of that dog. Dog food. Rat poison. Marie and her mother stopped their own conversation then—which had only concerned which would be the best day to go to the farmer's market that weekend, Saturday or Sunday—to listen.

"Hamburger," one of the women said. "Salt it."

"Hey!" Marie's mother had shouted—so loudly that Marie pulled the receiver away from her ear. "We CAN HEAR YOU! We're calling the police!"

Then the women were gone.

"When are we going to the pool?" Richie asked.

"First we're watching astronauts," Marie said. "Remember?

"Oh," Richie said.

It wasn't just on the telephone, she knew, with Richard. Richie truly hadn't seemed excited by the liftoff, or the astronauts, or the idea of men walking on the moon, even at first, and the longer it took for the big liftoff day, the wearier Richie had grown of hearing about it. He would have preferred a cartoon or a comic book about rockets to the real thing. And Marie would have preferred to have Richard there, explaining the importance of all this to him since she did not, herself, feel any more excited than Richie.

She had never thought that any of this was worth the risk.

"Who's on the moon?" Richie had asked when he first heard that "we" were going to the moon, and Marie thought it was the best question she'd heard anyone ask since this whole business started. *Who do we hope to meet on the moon?*

"No one," she'd said.

"Then why are we going?" Richie asked.

"I don't know," Marie told him. But then she thought of Richard and how, if he could hear her, he'd be disappointed, and she added, "Well, because it's important. No one has done it before."

If there were other reasons, she didn't know what those were.

She had, of course, seen photographs of the moon.

And it was nothing.

It was desolate and dusty, ancient and isolated. At best, the astronauts would land there to confirm this.

But what if they found something they didn't expect, weren't meant to find?

Then the disaster no one could ever imagined would begin to happen.

And what if they simply never got there? Then the moon would just be up there as it always had been, and those three astronauts on their way to it would be ashes gently falling back to Earth or left up there to orbit their nothingness forever.

8

The lifeguard attended West Mission Hills High. She had a lot of friends. She was popular. She was social. Someone had taken a photograph of the choir singing in June behind the graduating seniors, and several of the sopranos were laughing together, inappropriately, during the "Star Spangled Banner," and the lifeguard was one of them.

But those who knew her from high school, who read these articles (which they all did) knew that, although the lifeguard wasn't *un*popular, she wasn't a member of the most popular clique of kids—the ones who lived in big houses, had cars of their own, pools in their backyards, and no reason to take on summer jobs like lifeguarding at swim clubs.

Still, her popularity would be blamed.

She'd always been inattentive.

She'd failed her first try at her driver's license because she'd run over an orange cone while attempting to parallel park. She'd lost her Western Civilization textbook.

Worse accusations would be made:

She had a hangover. She was hanging out with some stoner who played the electric guitar. They smoked marijuana together. That's why she kept her eyes hidden behind those aviators.

She didn't like children.

She *hated* children.

She only took a lifeguard's job to show off her legs and her tan. She had no interest guarding the lives of the children swimming around below her, swimmers who were young and helpless and counting on her to save them.

She hadn't even noticed that the rope between the deep end and the shallow end of the pool had not been replaced in the two hours since the swim meet had ended.

9

Their hands were stamped, they were in the tunnel, and Richie knew he was almost there. The sound of the water. The sweet-clean-poison smell. The blue rippling sky-deeper-and-greener-and-bluer-than-sky just beyond the end of the tunnel, just past the chain-link fence and the gate with its complicated latch—which, last summer, Richie couldn't open without help, but he'd learned the trick to it since then, how you had to twist the pin at the same time you pulled up the latch.

Danny, the snack bar man, had taught him how to do it one day, which was exactly what Richie would do with Alex when he got old enough. He would teach his brother how to open the gate so he wouldn't have to wait for someone to do it for him to get into the pool.

They were almost there. In only a few minutes Richie would be in the pool with the other children. His whole body would be like it felt to be *made* out of water, free, swimming away and leaving yourself and all the walking and sitting and standing behind you, always stuck on the ground without ever having the wind pick you up and pull you over the sidewalk or letting you float with your feet off the floor from one room in your house to another with your arms parting the air around you so you were smoothly turning the corner from your bedroom to the bathroom while lying flat on your stomach, drifting and being pulled along at the same time instead of just having to walk everywhere on your feet, never being able to lie down between the ceiling and the floor and just rest there, unless you were in bed or lying on the couch.

In the rest of the world there was never any floating. Unless you were a ghost.

But the pool took away your body while you were still in it—the hovering, the drifting, the flying-with-no-wings.

The red-haired girl had passed them already, carrying that towel he'd seen flapping out of the basket between her handlebars. She was already out of the tunnel because she didn't have to wait for Richie's mother, who was holding Alex and moving slowly because Alex was getting heavy.

But Richie wasn't that far behind her. They were already in the middle of the tunnel. Almost there. Soon they would be in the grassy place behind the fence, close enough to the pool to hear the water splashing. All they had to do now was find a chair for his mom, who would sit in it and pull Richie's T-shirt off over his head and tie the lace of his swim trunks tighter. Then she would tell him to be careful, to mind all the rules, because she would be watching. Yes, she would let him go to the shallow end by himself like Daddy had promised, but she would be watching!

Then the light from the other side of the tunnel made Richie have to close his eyes and open them again. When he opened them he saw—

No.

No!

Mrs. Friedlander was coming out of the women's locker room. She was wearing a rubber cap with rubber flowers on her head, but Richie recognized her. She was looking both ways, like she was at the end of a block and about to cross, but Richie was afraid that she was looking for someone to talk to.

Richie was afraid Mrs. Friedlander would see his mom.

He pulled his mother's hand harder, to hold her back, where they couldn't be seen, and his mother looked down at his hand hurting hers and asked, "What are you doing, Richie?"

And then—

No—

"Oh, *hello there*," Mrs. Friedlander called out.

10

"Bethany," Steve said. "No one has to say anything if they'd prefer—"

But Bethany wasn't done with me.

She leaned toward Steve so fast he flinched. She shouted, "The *fuck* no one has to say anything! We've all talked and talked and talked and talked and talked. What right does she have to just sit here and listen and then show up to a meeting drunk?"

Bethany's right hand fluttered around her face for a few seconds before it fell dead in her lap. She inhaled and, in a lower and quieter voice, said, "I'm so sorry, Steve. But Sarah *owes* us. Sarah's got *secrets. Sarah's* got *stories.* And I for one want to hear all the gory details." She looked straight into my eyes before I could look back down at my knee and said, "Come on, *Sarah*! *Come on!* We paid to see a show tonight, and by God—"

"Bethany!" Steve said. He looked helpless. He bent over to pick up the book that had fallen out of his lap when he stood up, and I thought I saw him wince. Back pain. Or hip. Steve had problems with his eyesight. The large print in that book made the book twice as thick as anyone else's. He sat back down, the burden of it balancing on his knees.

Bethany sat on her hands. Maybe they were shaking, but her voice was steady. She looked around the circle without looking at me as she spoke, her tone changing to reasonable familiarity. She said to the circle, "Hey, come on. Don't you all know all about my baby? Like we all know how Nathan cracked his brother in the face with a baseball bat and how Terry forgot to go to his mother's funeral, right?"

A few nodded. I heard someone whisper, "It's true."

"So," Bethany went on, "all I want to know is what is *Sarah's* story? I want to hear it before I read about it in the *Littleton Gazette.*" She laughed then, a little. "Don't we all?"

Margo, a woman my mother's age, began to chew on her thumbnail. Steve opened his mouth, but didn't speak. Bethany stood up then and shouted, directly at me, "Spit it out, *SARAH.*"

"Stop!" Steve said—just loudly enough to startle everyone but Bethany. "Stop it!"

Bethany said, "I'm sorry," but she didn't sit back down.

Steve stuffed his huge book into his camouflage backpack. He glanced at his watch and said, "Okay. We're done for tonight. But if anyone would like to stick around and have coffee, that's fine. We just need to be out of the basement before the youth group gets here in thirty minutes. In the meantime, let's not forget: one day at a time. Be kind to yourselves. Okay? Be kind to each other. Let us pray."

We folded our hands and bowed our heads and everyone, it seemed, except for me mumbled along in unison with Steve as he recited the prayer with which these meetings began and ended: *God grant me the serenity to accept the things I cannot change, the courage to change the things I can, and the wisdom to know the difference.*

Four

10

No.

No!

Richie's head screamed NO as he felt his mother slow down, restrain him, use her weight to keep him from rushing her toward the end of the tunnel, which they'd almost reached before Mrs. Friedlander saw them.

But he had to stop because he knew that if he kept tugging his mother she might stumble. She could fall down. And then Alex would fall with her. And they would get hurt, and it would be his fault, and then he would wish forever that he had never wanted to go to the pool.

Richie didn't know what the word *guilt* meant yet, but he'd felt it, and didn't want to feel it again.

Once, in kindergarten, he told Mary Hatcher that he thought the doll she'd brought to school for show-and-tell was ugly. Which was true. It had ratty orange hair and was dirty on its cheeks, and the dress it wore had holes in it and also loose threads hanging from it. But then he saw the look on Mary Hatcher's face, and how her lip started to move, and how she could barely say anything because she was trying so hard not to cry, but she still managed to tell Richie, "She is my grandma's doll."

Everybody knew that Mary Hatcher's grandma was dead.

Dead like his own grandmother, who used to give him chalky peppermint candies in the backyard while she pinned wet clothes to a rope and wear a pink housedress with big pockets filled with clothespins and chalky peppermints.

And then (there was no use trying to avoid it now) Mrs. Friedlander was standing between Richie and Alex and his mother and the end of the tunnel.

"Here's Mrs. Friedlander," Richie's mother said to Richie.

But Richie already knew this.

Still, he nodded. To Be Polite.

"Say hi to Mrs. Friedlander, Richie," his mother said.

"Hi," Richie said, looking up at the old lady's wrinkly face.

But it was too far above him, that face. He couldn't keep his neck bent back like that for very long, so he looked down at her feet, which were spotted and bony and bare.

Then he felt the old woman's hand on his head, her fingers spread out around it, like she was going to twist a lid off a jar. She asked, "How are these little guys doing? Are they having a fun summer so far?"

She was asking his mother, so Richie didn't need to answer. Except she was also asking him, it seemed, because his mother said, "How are you doing, Richie? Can you tell Mrs. Friedlander?"

He was forced to look up at her face again, but before he did he saw over her shoulder the sun bouncing off the water slide, and he heard the laughter and the splashing of the children in the pool—so close to him that not only could he hear how happy they were, he could feel it. In his eyes. Like tears.

Another a splash. Someone had jumped into the pool from the side of it, and Richie could feel that, too—the way the pure cool blue absorbed you.

He heard his mother say something to Mrs. Friedlander about how Richie was overly excited about the moon that morning, which wasn't true, and then Mrs. Friedlander said something about saying a prayer for those brave men.

And, yes, Alex was getting big, wasn't he?

And, yes, Richie had passed his Tadpole class, so now he could reach and pull and kick.

"And I can go into the shallow end without a grown-up!" Richie said, snapping back into himself with the feeling of a rubber band on the back of your neck.

He looked at his mother, who wouldn't look at him.

"Well, that must make you happy, Richie!" Mrs. Friedlander said. "But you be careful, okay?"

He looked up at her then. His eyes moved from her wrinkled face to the rubber flowered cap on her head.

Why did they have to talk to Mrs. Friedlander here in the tunnel between the parking lot and the pool anyway? She only lived four houses away! Almost every day she walked past their front yard with her dog Bingo on a yellow leash. But you couldn't play with Bingo the way you could with other dogs because Bingo wasn't used to children. Bingo was nervous. You never knew what Bingo might do. Bingo might wag his tail and be happy, or Bingo might bite you.

Richie's mother and Mrs. Friedlander asked and answered the same questions they always did. (How are you? Fine. How are you? Fine.) But just when they were done answering those question his mother started talking about something funny that had happened on their block. A squirrel in a bird box? Mrs. Friedlander laughed.

Then Mrs. Friedlander had some story of her own about the antics of a squirrel, except that her story went on and on and on and on, and Richie wished that Alex would start to try to twist out of their mother's arms so she'd want to find a lounge chair and put him down. Instead, Alex just stared at Mrs. Friedlander's swim cap, the rubber flowers. He looked worried, but Richie could tell that his brother was too interested in those flowers to start to fuss.

"I'm so glad," Mrs. Friedlander said, "to see these healthy boys! I sure miss my own little boys! I wish Chum had opened this swim club when mine were little cubs like yours and I could've brought them here. You're making memories, Marie. You'll cherish these memories forever, believe me. Time flies. You just can't know how quickly it's all over until it's all over!"

Richie pictured an alarm clock with wings in the sky above the pool.

Richie's mother made a sad sound, but Richie knew his mother didn't like it when Mrs. Friedlander talked about time passing. He'd heard his mother tell her friend Sandy on the telephone, not knowing that Richie was standing around the corner and could hear, that the old lady Patty Friedlander a few doors down was always going on and on and on about how much she missed her sons—but whenever they came to visit, Patty Friedlander wouldn't let them in the house. His mother said, "They stand around for half an hour or so with a bouquet on her porch and their mother will only eventually open the screen door wide enough to grab it."

Richie knew for a fact that nothing Mrs. Friedlander said about her little boys was true.

There were no little boys.

There were, instead, two men who drove their cars into her driveway now and then, wore suits, and worked somewhere Richie's father also wanted to work. His father had said to Richie once, when a long blue car passed their house while they were backing out of the driveway, "One of the Friedlander brothers. Those two are making money hand over fist over there with Uncle Todd."

Richie was plenty old enough to understand that little boys grew up to be men, but he also knew (although he didn't know how he knew) that these men had never been Mrs. Friedlander's little boys. They didn't love her.

Richie stood up straighter when he heard Mrs. Friedlander say, "Have fun!"—which must have meant that she was saying goodbye, but first she had to smile and touch Alex's hair—which he hardly even had, just a brown tuft at the top. But even though everything Mrs. Friedlander did was still in slow motion, Richie knew by the way she cooed at the tuft that she was going to leave them alone now and that soon they would no longer be talking to her in the tunnel, but they would be walking *out* of the tunnel together, and then—

Then!

9

"Mommmmmm, izzzz worrrrr mmmmayyybe you shuuuuuuld . . ."

After this, there was a long pause filled with the sound of miniature wheels spinning or waves washing up in slow motion on a sandy beach.

Despite the broken answering machine, I recognized the voice slurring from the miniature tape-recording cartridge hidden somewhere inside of it as my sister's. I couldn't talk to her now. She would be able to tell I'd been drinking. And she'd tell Mom. And I hadn't moved from Michigan to New Hampshire to have the two of them tell me what to do. Even when they were right. Even when I knew they were.

Especially when I knew they were, or when they had been.

Wolfie and I wouldn't last, they'd said. If I moved to New Hampshire to be with him, instead of staying in Michigan to be with *them*, I'd end up drinking again, and there'd be no one around who cared.

After I understood that Chicago wasn't a big enough city or far enough away from Michigan to blend inconspicuously into the blustering sleet and the background churning of that lake, but after I'd met Wolfie on that beach, I went back to Michigan for a few weeks. I stayed with my sister, and together we visited my mother at Springbrook Manor every afternoon, where, at my mother's bedside, the two of them would paint my future in ever oilier and darker layers of gray. Once, and only once, my sister said to me in the car as we pulled out of the nursing home parking lot into the rest of the world, "You might just want to think about sticking around, for Mom." When I didn't respond she, unfortunately, went on. "She's been through a lot, you know. Her life has been full of fucking trouble, and now she's getting ready to die." When I still didn't respond she repeated, "A lot of trouble." Next, to the silence between us in the haze left behind by the thousands of cigarettes she'd smoked in the claustrophobic space, she said, "Because of you."

I opened my mouth.

But I was breathing too hard to speak.

After a few miles spent like this I managed to ask, "Did you just tell me that Mom's had so much trouble—because of *me*?"

I laughed, and even to me the noise coming out of me sounded only an inch or two away from hysteria.

But she didn't even seem to need to think about it.

"Yeah," she said.

And then, as if she could not possibly have meant what I'd thought she had, she went on to tell me that Mom always perked up when I came home, and she talked about me all the time, and it would be fun, really, if the two of us could go up and visit her together every other day or so. The nurses and the aides were really a lot of fun. Also my nieces and nephew would like to have me around and I could stay with them until I found my own place.

She could not have meant that I'd brought "the trouble" on myself.

No.

She was too much of a feminist for that.

And we were long past any questioning of gratitude or blame for what happened after that, having had several years of court-ordered therapy in which to discuss, and bury forever, all that.

Then I calmed down and just stared out the window as my sister told me a tenth time about how she understood my impulse to run off to the woods of New Hampshire with a handsome older man that I'd just met . . . but, seriously, you don't have to be a rocket scientist to predict how that's going to turn out."

"Oh, tell me then."

We were idling outside my sister's two-car garage by then, the doors of which they never opened because what was behind them was so crammed with old patio furniture and bicycles and boxes of broken toys that it would all spill out onto the driveway if they did.

"Honestly? You want me to tell you what will happen, honestly."

I wanted to say no, but I didn't.

"Well, you're gonna start drinking again. It's going to be fun and harmless at first and you and this Wolfie will have a grand time for about three months, and in about a year you'll be drinking first thing every morning."

I'd asked for that.

"Thank you."

I erased her message on our broken answering machine and turned to the refrigerator, took out the only thing besides whatever it was that was leafy and green and blurred and stinking and furred in the crisper, a can of Diet Coke.

Had Wolfie packed the margarine and the brick of cheddar cheese along with the VCR and the stereo when he left? Or had I eaten a cheese sandwich last night? If I had, I couldn't remember it. But I also had no memory of either of us throwing the answering machine against the wall, although one of us apparently did.

I held the can, cold and sweaty, to my right temple, where the throbbing had moved since I got out of bed—from the center of my brain to the side of it—before I cracked it open and took a sip.

Then I remembered the bottle of gin I'd bought on the way home from the AA meeting.

I hadn't even known, then, that three days later, Wolfie still would not be back.

He'd only called once that I knew of, leaving a message on the warped tape, sounding like Linda Blair: "I hope you're okay, but—bye." His message had been followed by one I vaguely understood to be from Bethany. It didn't sound like her, on that tape, but she said something about breakfast for dinner again. Either she was inviting me over once more or she was permanently rescinding that invitation.

I didn't remember giving Bethany my phone number, but apparently, I had.

I'd hidden the bottle of gin inside one of my winter boots, pressing it down into the dark wool where it waited for me in the back of my closet behind the dress I'd bought to wear to the courthouse to marry Wolfie a hundred years ago.

8

Richard rarely ordered hard liquor on an airplane, but that day he did, perhaps inspired by the sagging, snoring older man beside him (whose sweat and suit and very presence smelled piercingly of whiskey), and also by the stewardess's blindingly white smile.

Not long after that stewardess brought him his little plastic cup of Coke (mostly ice cubes), she bent over the seat in which the older man snored to ask Richard if she could do anything else for him, revealing a lovely V of cleavage. "There's plenty of time for a quick one if you're interested!" she said.

Richard had no way of knowing whether or not she'd meant to

sound like she was offering him more than a miniature bottle of hard liquor, but the flight would be over soon, after which he had to go straight to downtown Dallas, so he'd never know. He asked for some scotch to pour into his Coke, although by then his Coke was mostly just its own melted ice cubes.

"Lovely!" she said and stood up.

She was just doing her job.

When she returned with the little bottle, Richard took it from her perfectly manicured hand and swiftly splashed it into the watery ice cubes.

He sipped. That warmth on his soft palate. The sense it gave him of childhood in winter. His blue wool blanket. His mother's hand on his forehead. A tablespoon of cough medicine.

He looked out the plane's window.

It was so green down there, and the atmosphere was completely clear between the oval window of his plane and the forest beneath him that he felt he could've counted the leaves on the trees, the needles in the pines. All of it, from the sky, looked waxy, and beautiful, and strange.

He thought about the astronauts.

My God, what must they be seeing, looking down?

He wondered if, having seen the world from that perspective, you would ever feel like a mortal again. Could you simply cross a busy street without thinking about how ant-like and unimportant you were—how lost you were down here, from up there.

Could you ever again do anything and not feel bored, empty, like you'd left yourself behind when you came home?

7

And then when he was close enough to hear the sound of the water splashing and the shouting of the children swimming in the pool, after they were almost to the entrance, Richie's mother remembered something she wanted to tell the snack bar man as he passed them on his way out of the tunnel.

"Oh, Danny," his mother said. "Hi there. I wanted to ask you a question—"

Danny stopped and turned around, and then (*oh no*) Richie's mother stopped, too. She and the snack bar man talked forever after that—something about whether or not his mother was still growing all those roses in their backyard. Danny was telling Richie's mother that, yes, she was, and that *you should come over and see.* That his mother had more varieties of roses than ever—some of them really exotic, or just invented (which puzzled Richie, the idea of a rose being *invented*), and then Richie's mother said that, actually, would Danny please tell his mother that she would call soon, that she wanted to come over, that she certainly would never have the kind of green thumb Danny's mother had, but she'd like to start doing that kind of thing with her own garden, and that of all the gardens she'd ever seen, Mrs. Applegate's was the most inspiring, and that she'd love to see what she was doing differently this summer and to ask her some questions about how to get started herself the next year, since it was too late in the season now to get to anything serious, but she could at least start to dream!

Danny said that his mother would love to mentor Richie's mother—whatever that meant. And then his mother started talking about a particular rose she'd seen in Mrs. Applegate's garden last year and how it had been called a White Circus.

Richie decided to take a step toward the tunnel's exit.

A small one.

The blue light at the end of it might catch his mother's eye so she'd forget about the roses, which Richie remembered seeing some other summer, and not liking. They'd been spaced far apart from each other, and each one had its own little nametag, and they were colors you wouldn't necessarily want a rose to be—like, there was one that was brown and some small orange sherbet-colored ones. And Mrs. Applegate had gone on and on, just like his mother and Danny went on and on, and she'd taken them into the garage, shown his mother some spray bottles and bags of rocky dust, explaining and explaining, and Richie had been so happy and relieved when Alex woke up in his stroller screaming, and they had to hurry to leave—even though Mrs. Applegate said that if Richie wasn't afraid of dogs, she'd let Mutton out.

Mutton might jump, though. And maybe Richie's mother would rather not have a dirty dog jumping on her clean little boy.

Then Richie didn't want to leave after all. He hadn't known there was a dog. He wanted to see the dog, but Alex kept fussing and they *would have to come back*. Which they never did, so Richie did not know if there was really ever a dog.

"Okay, Mrs. Manning! See you soon!"

Danny's hair was shaggy. His Jolly Rogers T-shirt was tucked into his jeans. He was a skinny, tall man, who might actually not have been quite a man yet.

"Bye!" Richie said.

"See ya, Rich!" Danny Applegate said.

But then (*oh no*) Richie's mother started to ask about his plans for after graduation.

Then Richie stopped listening. His ears were making a hollow pounding sound beyond which he could now barely hear the laughter coming from beyond the tunnel, and the whoosh of someone moving smoothly down the slide, the splash that followed, when the child who'd been sliding was tossed by the end of the slide into the water—

Because that's what that sound felt like:

Like the slide was throwing you away, so that no matter how

many times you went down it, finding yourself thrown out of it, you were always surprised by the sudden release and the way you started to gasp for air just before you sank, and then how you held your breath whether you wanted to or not as you started to thrash your way back to the surface, and then you had to dog-paddle to the ladder, climb out, and then maybe you would head straight back to stand in line for the slide again, even though your heart was still racing and if you weren't so out of breath you were afraid you might cry.

He looked behind him and saw the girl with the black braid from the entrance in her chair with her clipboard and stamp staring at him.

Right at him.

But like she couldn't see him.

He wondered if he should wave. But he didn't because he had the feeling that she wasn't trying to see him, that she was trying to see something *inside* of him, and a wave would just confuse her.

He looked away from her and squinted at the light just beyond the tunnel. He almost thought he could see the blur of a beach ball sailing through the air above the water. He could definitely see the ponytail of the lifeguard on her white throne. Above her, in the paler blue, he was pretty sure he saw the rocket ship carrying those astronauts, who were looking down, wishing (Richie imagined) that they could be children again, on Earth, ready to dive into blue water and to float and sink and rise and gasp and splash and jump and fly down the slide, be tossed into the water under a sun and a sky with no clouds, with a huge ball of fire over it, with a space ship in it headed for the moon, which, at that moment, was invisible, Richie knew, although he was pretty sure he could see the white shadow of it in that blue, too.

6

The lifeguard didn't notice the missing rope that afternoon, which had not been, as it usually was, strung from one side of the pool to the other. It was a waxy, thick blue-and-white rope held afloat in the center of the pool by three red buoys.

Its purpose was to separate the deep end from the shallow end.

But that day no one remembered to replace it after it was taken down for the swim meet, which had been delayed so that the swimmers could stay home to watch the liftoff on TV.

Neil Armstrong, Michael Collins, and Buzz Aldrin had been launched by a 363-foot-tall rocket from Kennedy Space Center into the sky. They would, by the next day, enter the moon's orbit, transfer into the lunar module (renamed *Eagle* from *Snoopy*), and begin to descend into the Sea of Tranquility.

You'll remember this day for the rest of your lives.

You are a witness to history.

But, in another decade, many of those children would have no recollection whatsoever of having witnessed anything at all that day.

The Jolly Rogers won the swim meet.

It was their first victory of the season.

They got a trophy—which had been purchased by Chum Rogers together with the owner of the Forest Hills Country Club's swim team, the Sharkfins, to be engraved with the name of whichever of the teams won the meet.

The team members wrapped themselves in towels and gathered around their coach with the trophy for photos taken not only by the swim team members' mothers but also by someone from the local newspaper.

That's how big a day this was at the Jolly Rogers Swim Club.

Nothing had been engraved on the trophy yet, since no one could have known in advance who would win the meet, but the trophy was large and bright, and the bursts of light that bounced off it from the flashbulbs of the many Kodaks aimed in its direction ruined most of the photos taken by anyone except the newspaper.

Dozens of prints came back from PhotoMatic (which had just opened and was already beginning to put the other photo developers in Mission Hills out of business) with no trace of the smiling swimmers or any trophy.

Blank. Blurred. Or just, at the center of many of the glossy squares, one exploded star ricocheting off it back into the lens of the camera from which it had come.

Holding those photos in their hands after opening the envelope from PhotoMatic, studying them closely, trying to find some trace of the swimmers and their smiles and their trophy captured in them, but finding nothing, it would seem to many who'd been there that, in fact, nothing at all had happened that day, and they'd seen it with their own eyes, held the proof of it in their own hands before throwing it away.

5

Until Richie Manning drowned at the swim club, Danny Applegate had felt like everything in the world was perfect as long as you didn't turn the television on, which, unfortunately, his mother kept doing, and then she would start going on and on about riots and cults and Vietnam, and then his parents would argue about President Nixon, about Huey Newton, about communism, about the draft, about women wanting to be more equal than men.

His parents agreed on nothing when they were in front of the television, whether or not his dad was chasing his mom around the kitchen table an hour later trying to pinch her as she giggled.

Their friends were no longer friends with one another.

Even from church.

A few nuns his mother knew from the hospital where she volunteered had been arrested outside the state capitol building, protesting the war. Danny's mother had shown him a photograph of them in the *Mission Hills Herald*, wearing their habits with their hands cuffed behind their backs, being led to a van that said POLICE on its side, although that van looked to Danny like the van that patrolled their neighborhood sometimes, in search of lost, stray dogs.

Sister Lucianne and Sister Beatrice became famous for a few months after that—partly because just as many people who admired them hated them.

They were brave. They were traitors. They'd been put in handcuffs! Nuns! They'd been given the soft treatment because they were nuns. They should rot in prison. Our boys are dying over there. They just want to save lives.

End the war. Win the war.

Across the street from the Applegates' house, there was a large old Victorian house—pink, with a fire escape that wound from the ground up to the attic, with a platform outside a window on every floor—which the owner couldn't sell because of "the neighborhood," so he rented it out, and about a dozen hippies moved in, and now a giant pink and yellow peace signed faced the Applegates' picture window.

To him the new neighbors seemed like grown-ups wearing costumes. Tie-dyed shirts. Bandanas. The women had hair so straight and long it looked like it was made of water. The men had frizzy beards. Everyone wore beads.

When they first moved in, Dan had hoped some interesting music might come from their house, but they seemed only to have one record, the soundtrack to *The Graduate*, which they played over and over again all day.

A few days before Richie Manning drowned, Danny's mother

told him she wanted him to come with her across the street to properly greet these new neighbors.

There had been many such neighborly greetings in Danny's life, always involving banana bread wrapped in waxed paper, which his mother would ask him to carry, and which always felt soggy and heavy and like an animal trying to keep still, perhaps out of terror, in his hands, breathing.

He'd followed his mother across the street to the peace sign. They climbed the front porch and edged around a pile of bicycles propped up against a plaid couch, and his mother pressed her finger into the doorbell's black eye.

They heard no sound coming from inside the house, so they waited a few seconds before his mother knocked. Then they heard voices—and the sounds of people who'd been motionless beginning to move around. Chair legs scraping against floors. Children jumping out of bunk beds. A toilet flushed. But no one came to the door or called out to them.

They stood there for as long as seemed polite, and then his mother turned to Danny and shrugged. They left the banana bread on the plaid couch, on which there was now, somehow, a cat, asleep.

Those hippies let a lot of dogs run loose in the neighborhood before they moved away. But they never caused any other trouble Danny ever heard about.

4

"Off you go," Becca's stepfather said as she wheeled her bike from the driveway to the sidewalk to ride it to the pool for the first time. "Be careful. Follow all the rules that we talked about. And get yourself some lunch at the snack bar."

Becca still found it strange and miraculous that she could just get a hot dog or a grilled cheese sandwich without giving the snack bar guy any money. He just put it under her name, and a bill for it was paid by her stepfather. But she said yes, thank you, she would get lunch at the snack bar, and then she put her hands on the handlebars and her feet on the pedals, and soon she sailed, and her hair streamed behind her, and people waved at her from cars as they drove by, even though she was brand new to this neighborhood so none of these people knew her or that she was the daughter of their neighbor's new wife.

All the nice houses with their green lawns were lined up along the smooth sidewalk. Here, she didn't have to worry about dogs like in her old neighborhood, where sometimes no one owned them and they came out from around the sides of buildings and houses and even though you knew you weren't supposed to, you couldn't help yourself from running, and where she would not have been allowed to ride a bike alone.

The dogs in West Mission Hills just sat quietly on front stoops and watched her pedal by on that summer day, on the way to the swim club, with a long flaming comet tail of red hair blowing around behind her.

3

That white cat crossed the street in front of the lifeguard so casually it seemed to express total faith in the lifeguard behind the wheel. She kept her foot on the brake for a long time after she'd already seen the cat climb the curb and make its way into a front lawn—headed, it seemed, for a bird feeder hanging from a tree branch.

The cat's shadow seemed to linger in front of her car in the street for longer than it should have. And the lifeguard didn't even want to run over that shadow. She glanced in her rearview mirror and saw, riding a bike down the sidewalk beside her, a little girl with long red hair, pedaling a light blue bike. A towel flapped from a wicker basket between her handlebars.

The bike was too big for the girl, but she was moving quickly and smoothly on it. Despite the awkwardness of standing while pedaling, that red-haired girl was, in fact, moving so quickly that the lifeguard could almost imagine her reaching the swim club before she did in her mother's rusty Duster.

But that little girl wouldn't be let through the gate until the swim meet was over and the lifeguard was seated above the pool. No one could swim at Jolly Rogers Swim Club without the lifeguard in attendance. And she was the lifeguard.

2

HUNDREDS ATTEND DROWNED BOY'S FUNERAL

There was, under the headline, a photograph of Marie and Richard Manning, their heads bent like heavy blossoms, walking out of Trinity Lutheran Church, following a casket.

Mrs. Manning wore a black dress with long sleeves. Mr. Manning wore a black suit with a thin tie that the newspaper photographs made look gray.

The pallbearers were four young men who made that casket look as light as an empty box.

But everyone who attended the funeral knew that the box wasn't empty.

Throughout the service, the casket was open in front of the altar, and Richie Manning inside it looked completely alive, while lying deathly still in the same black suit he'd worn months earlier as the ring bearer at his aunt's wedding.

Drowning being the kind of death that leaves a body unscarred and unbroken, even his kindergarten and Sunday school classmates (many even younger than Richie himself) were not afraid of seeing him being dead, and they proved willing—even eager—to be led past to wave goodbye up to him, or held up over him to look down at him and wave. One or two little girls even kissed his cheek and said, "I love you, Richie." And Richie's cheek, truthfully, was no colder than the cheeks of some of the living aunts and grandmother's those little girls had kissed in hospital beds.

No one seemed to know, and no one asked, where the younger brother was.

Little Alex was somewhere else in the church—in the nursery, perhaps, maybe with a relative. Or perhaps he had been left at home with a babysitter. They hoped so. What would be the point of bringing a child that age, who would only be confused and afraid, to a funeral to see his big brother laid out in a box, on an altar, with this gray flower arrangement photographed for the newspaper and the candles on the altar already having burned so far down by the time it was over (since the service was one of the longest that had ever been held at the church) that the wax had started to crawl away from them, sluglike.

Likely a child that age would remember nothing anyway. So maybe it made no difference—but what if he *did* remember?

What if his first memory was of his mother, during the minister's benediction, stumbling up from her seat in the front pew, yanking her arm out of the hand of her husband, who was trying to hold her back, to keep her from throwing herself on their son's body, from diving head first into that too-large casket (why hadn't a child's size been made?), lifting his dead brother up in her arms, bending her head down to her chest, seeming to be trying to listen for a heartbeat while the father stood paralyzed.

After his wife shook her arm out of his grip, Mr. Manning just sat back down in the pew and didn't rise again. It was as if, once she'd slipped his grip, he lost all hope of every bringing her back.

But several other men jumped up from their pews and ran to Marie Manning, and although none of them tried to pull her son away from her, they bent down over the mother and the child she was holding and they eased her down to her knees at the altar before she handed the boy up to one of the men.

By then, no one could hear the organist, if he was even playing. And the minister just stood there with his arms in the air, not finishing what he'd perhaps just started to say before Mrs. Manning tried to take back her son.

The pants he'd worn as ring bearer a few months earlier were a bit too short for him by the time he died.

1

Then, as they were just stepping out of the tunnel, into pool light and splashing, the lifeguard blew her whistle, bright and sharp, slicing straight through the center of the sound of water, before shouting, "Adult Swim, kids! Get out of the water! Fifteen minutes!"

Richie felt his whole body sag and wrinkle up like a balloon the day after a party.

No.

No.

He stopped, although his mother tugged on his hand.

There was no point now.

Adult Swim.

Which lasted forever.

The children had to wait forever to get into the pool while the adults lapped around in the water in slow motion, forever.

"Please, Richie," his mother said, and pulled on his hand harder. "Don't sulk. You're a big boy. You can wait fifteen minutes until

Adult Swim is over to get in the pool. I don't want any *behavior* from you. Do you understand?"

When his mother said the word "behavior," she touched the back of Richie's neck, right below where his skeleton's skull would be if he was a Halloween decoration or a picture in a book about bones.

He knew what that squeeze meant:

Do *not* fuss, whine, or complain.

It meant:

Do not feel how you are feeling.

It's the touch she gave Richie in church when he got bored. And at the doctor when he was about to get a shot. She did it when they had to stand too long in a line at the grocery store. She did it whenever they arrived at the pool as Adult Swim was starting, which was *almost every time*!

"It's not fair!" Richie said. It was a statement. He didn't whine it, but then he whined and said, "We *just got here*!"

"Richie, don't start. Come on. By the time we get settled, you'll be in the pool. Adult Swim is only fifteen minutes."

Five

1

Fifteen minutes!

Why?

Why did they need Adult Swim at all?

Adults could do anything they wanted whenever they wanted to do it!

Adult Swim was mostly just some old people dragging themselves over some black lines sadly and some moms sitting at the edge dangling their legs off the side of the pool, talking about boring things while their children waited, and waited, and waited, behind a chain-link fence.

All day, the pool got farther away the closer he got to it!

His whole life away.

His mother said, "You'll be in the pool in no time."

But there was no such thing as No Time.

Time was that paste holding everything together, slowing everything down, except for recess and certain cartoons that finished so fast you just started watching them when they were already over.

Richie hated Time.

It was the reason everything was always already over before it started.

2

So it was that Richard Manning allowed his son to be put in the ground for all of eternity in the same kind of casket anyone might be buried in, one that had likely come off an assembly line in a factory in some dismal Southern state, shipped up north in the trailer of a semi to be stored away, just waiting for some ordinary death of some ordinary boy, one who'd died some kind of death that had come as no surprise to anyone.

After nearly a year had passed since his son's burial, he woke up one night not from one of his nightmares of being locked underground, shouting to be let out a box too small to breathe inside, he dreamed instead that he was inside a box that was too big. He wasn't trapped now: he was lost. He woke up gasping for breath, and when he caught it again he looked over to see Marie staring at him from her side of the bed, staring at him with the unblinking dead-straight gaze of an animal. Her face was illuminated by a crack of moonlight slipping itself between the window shade and sill. She looked like the ghost of the mother of a dead child.

And, Richard realized, he despised her.

And he blamed her.

"It's your fault," he said in the direction of that ghost-mother's face.

"How dare you," she said.

How long had she been awake?

Had she ever slept at all?

She did not sound as if she'd been sleeping. She sounded as if she'd been waiting.

"How dare you," she said again, flatly and calmly. "Who was flying around the country while I was taking care of—"

"*Taking care* . . . Well, that didn't work out too well!"

Richard was surprised to hear his own voice saying this so confidently.

He hadn't blamed Marie for the drowning yet. Had he?

No. He blamed her that their son, in that cheap piece of shit, was never going to be able to rest.

"You and your fucking family," he said. "The Pulaskis. Proud to be paupers!"

"What the hell are you talking about?" she asked him before she got out of bed and put on her robe.

"You and the whole Pulaski 'I hate waste' club."

Waste, hating it, was something Marie's mother had said whenever someone didn't finish eating whatever horrible thing she'd dumped for them on a plate. It was something Marie herself said now, not even seeming to realize that "I hate waste" was her now-dead mother's line.

Richard repeated it, in a falsetto, like a dead woman: "'I just hate waste!'"

Then he chuckled, like a killer in a movie.

Marie stood beside the bed, looking down at him in the bruise-colored light of pre-dawn seeping under their bedroom curtain right beside the fading moonlight, and there was no mistaking what her expression was saying, but she said it out loud anyway:

"What I hate is you."

3

Those who were the quickest to forgive the lifeguard were those who'd attended Our Lady of the Roses with her every Sunday through all the years since her parents had moved to Mission Hills. Their own children had attended catechism classes and Sunday school with her. She'd performed in the annual Nativity plays—beginning as a lamb in a woolly jumpsuit that her mother made for her (using stuffing cut out of an old bedspread) and ending as the Virgin Mary, wearing a pale blue robe (a white bedsheet her mother had dyed).

She'd sung in the children's choir. She'd played handbells with the choir through several Advent seasons. At one Palm Sunday service, she'd performed a solo. Her voice trembled (perhaps she was thinking of her dead father), but it was lovely: *I am fully saved today, All my guilt is washed away . . .*

They'd watched the back of her blond head throughout her poor father's funeral.

He'd been a good man. A mailman. He'd died on a sidewalk in a snowstorm.

Some could even remember her baptism, seventeen years earlier. Back then, her parents had been strangers to them. They were old, it seemed, to be new parents of a newborn. They must have struggled for a long time before being blessed.

The day she was baptized, that new couple brought the lifeguard to the front of the church, to a basin wheeled there by an altar boy with blond curls and pink cheeks—who, until he was convicted a decade later of raping a child (his cousin) under the age of twelve, had appeared to many of members of the congregation to be brain-damaged, or an angel.

That day, the lifeguard had been the size of a loaf of bread. But she was dressed in a lace gown that had been passed down through generations of the lifeguard's mother's line, having been sewn by Mary Doyle, a great-great-great-grandmother of the lifeguard—a woman who'd lived and died in a cottage in Ireland (like so many of their own great-great-great-grandmothers) and then had been buried with no gravestone too close to the sea. During one rainy winter, the cemetery flooded, and the woman's coffin, bearing her corpse, had been washed away, so the only proof that the woman had ever lived was that gown and a few stories passed down with it: how she'd dressed each of her eleven children (four of whom survived to adulthood, but only one of whom lived to have a child who would live to have a child who would live to have the child who gave birth to the mother of the lifeguard) for their baptisms.

And, miraculously, after a century of such baptisms, the gown was still pure white.

It was immaculate—not yellowed and without a single thread that appeared to be loose or frayed.

Many who were there that day looked closely at that gown.

Some said to others, "That gown should be in a museum. It would be worth a couple thousand dollars to an antiques dealer, easy!"

"Except that no one would ever sell something like that! Look at it!"

An intricate web of stitches sewn with the thinnest threads.

A college girl wrote an essay about it for the church newsletter:

Perhaps she stitched it by candlelight, or as the peat fire burned?

That girl had interviewed the congregation's newest mother about the gown in which her daughter had been baptized. There was a good story about that. The ancestress had woven it using a bobbin made from the hip bone of a goat.

The college girl who wrote about the gown had been home for the summer, working part-time for the church (mostly dusting pews), and her account was considered by many to be pure fiction, sentimental nonsense, a flight of fancy penned by a girl who should have been working at a dime store instead of wasting her time in college. Then, seventeen years after Richie Manning drowned, that same college girl, now Mrs. Anne Smith, would be the member of the congregation who most blamed the lifeguard.

She was by then married to a police officer, and she had a kindergartner herself, who'd attended West Mission Elementary School with Richie Manning. And ever since that boy's drowning, that daughter had woken up screaming every night, and whenever Mrs. Smith ran to comfort her, her child's bedroom filled with the scent of strawberries.

One day she would write a story about this for the Our Lady of the Roses website.

4

The sky was completely clear that afternoon. It was a soft and tame and pure sky-blue.

The pool was blue, too, but it was a completely different kind of blue.

Tropical Cove Electric Aqua Blue.

Above the pool, the sky's blue looked faded. Too many washings in too many institutional machines, like the hospital gown of a patient in a bed with a railing under too-bright fluorescent lighting. Nothing.

But the pool's blue was Richie Manning's favorite color.

All winter, while the pool was closed, he'd felt afraid he might forget it.

His favorite color.

And also his favorite smell.

Chlorine, his mother called it.

Richie didn't know what Chlorine was, just what it smelled like, so he thought of it as a flower in his grandmother's garden.

His grandmother grew flowers with strange names. Before she was put in a box and buried in the ground, she would point at a blossom and tell Richie to smell it.

He'd put his nose right in the middle of a flower and sniff.

The red ones smelled like knots of rope soaked in cherry Kool-Aid. The purple ones smelled like almost-burned waffles. The orange ones smelled like mushed bananas. The yellow ones smelled like cough medicine. The white ones smelled like cupcake frosting, but frosting mixed up with your father's shaving cream. The pink ones smelled like Fruit Loops left floating in the thin milk his mother liked because it made her skinny.

Skim Milk.

Skinny Milk.

Which was see-through.

So the chlorines would be the white ones and smell like new sheets or like the floor right after your mother mopped it.

And Richie Manning wanted the whole world to smell like that, and last summer, it did. After he swam in the pool all day, even after he took a bath and his mother washed his hair, he could smell it on the palms of his hands and on his pillowcase. He could especially smell it on his wrists, where he had his thinnest skin and could see right through himself to the tangles of blue thread in there that were his veins and some bones that were skinnier than the wishbones his mother kept from the turkey. They would snap them apart, and the one with the bigger half got the wish. That was always him.

Chlorines.

They would be the invisible flowers in a grandmother's garden, but you would know where they were growing because of their scent.

Even when he hadn't gone to the pool that summer for a whole week (mostly because his brother was still drinking milk from his mother, so they'd had to stay home) he could smell the chlorines under his wrist skin, which he'd learned to smell from watching his mother do this at the perfume counter at Steketee's downtown after the saleslady sprayed her. Even when he was angry that they hadn't been to the pool for a *week,* he knew the pool was still there when he smelled his wrists. Then he could still imagine himself again looking down at the shifty mirror of the water and the wobbling black lines painted under it.

He could picture the place, even in winter, where the shallow end turned into the deep end (where he'd never been), and how the water got darker there, and harder to understand then.

5

I couldn't blame Wolfie for the miscarriage. The doctor told us "these things happen" and "it's generally for the best," that if the baby hadn't escaped my body in a rush of blood, it might have been born damaged, deformed, dying or dead. "It's nature's way of—"

"Shut the fuck up," Wolfie said to the doctor before slamming his office door behind him, leaving me alone, still lying on a sheet of paper on a table, in that office.

When I got out to the parking lot, he was in his truck and had his hands on the steering wheel. He was staring straight ahead.

I couldn't blame Wolfie for the relapse.

I couldn't even blame him for the move to New Hampshire. I'd wanted to move to be with him.

Then he told me one night over a bowl of macaroni and cheese, after I was no longer pregnant and had started to drink again, that he felt like he was living with a ghost. Was I *ever* going to *talk* to him about *what I was thinking about*?

"Who even are you?" he asked, and then he stared at me, long and hard, as if waiting for an answer. He put his fork down in the bowl, hard, and then he put his face in his hands. "Why in the hell do I have to ask *my wife* who she is?"

He was, I realized then, a pathetic man.

A few weeks earlier, I'd watched him comb a matted clot of fur off the belly of a stray cat in the carport of our apartment building. From the window, seeing this, I knew long before it happened that this cat would bite or scratch him. When I saw Wolfie scrabble backward, holding his hand, I turned away from the window. He wore a bandage around his hand for a few days after that, but he never told me what had happened, and I didn't ask about the bandage.

Now, he was gone, and I had a bottle of gin. It was morning.

Then, suddenly, it was noon, and I was idling outside the Littleton Liquor & Wine Outlet in a downpour. My wipers stirred the water around on my windshield as I waited, until I realized that there was no point in waiting, that this storm was nowhere close to done, so I grabbed my purse and ran in the direction of the store's glass door, behind which a silvery light shone down from the ceiling onto the rows and rows of bottles, which sent back to the ceiling their own silvery light.

6

NO RUNNING—

That was the #1 Rule on the Jolly Rogers Swim Club Rule Board. And it was the rule that was most often broken.

The lifeguard blew her whistle whenever a child even so much as started to break the rule by taking such long, fast steps she knew that running would have to follow unless the child could fly.

When the lifeguard noticed Richie Manning, he was not yet running, but he was getting closer to it. She watched him. But he was not yet the child drowning in the middle of the pool. He was still just another kid moving too quickly over wet cement near the edge of the pool. He wanted to go down the slide, it seemed, and the older children were passing him, elbowing him out of the way, while the line grew longer and longer the longer it took him to get into the line.

Wasn't this the little boy she'd noticed a bit earlier being called out of the water by his mother?

That mother had been holding a younger child in her arms, standing at the edge of the pool, leaning down, calling to him as he pinwheeled in the water with his arms, drifting farther away from where his mother stood.

Either he couldn't hear her over the sound of the splashing and shouting, or he wanted to pretend he couldn't.

Then his mother must have shouted at him to stop, which he did, but he also frowned. His mother returned the frown and pointed to the stairs and either shouted or mouthed, "Get, out, now," while all around him the other children continued on with their swimming business. One punched a beach ball into the air, and that beach ball sailed over Richie Manning's head. A little red-haired girl jumped into the water near him, and a prismatic explosion obscured the lifeguard's vision of the mother and the boy for several seconds. When it cleared, that boy was pulling himself up the side of the pool with his arms instead of going up the stairs at which his mother was pointing.

He struggled over the concrete lip of it, and the lifeguard winced, thinking about that bare belly, with its tender flesh, scraping against the rough surface.

Then, they were gone, and the lifeguard saw that a little girl was about to dive into the shallow end, right above the Jolly Rogers Rule #2, stenciled onto the cement—NO DIVING IN SHALLOW END—and then the lifeguard wouldn't see that boy again until he started to run.

7

As well as the abrasion on the boy's torso, the pathologist noted two bruises on his body, both of which were quite recently acquired—one at the center of the left scapula and a nearly identical one directly between the clavicles, close to the base of his throat—but not so recently acquired that the flesh hadn't begun to discolor at the sites of the injuries.

Both bruises were the same shape and size (round, three inches in diameter), and appeared to the pathologist to be injuries one might expect to find as the result of blows from a small fist. Except that these bruises weren't jagged, as bruises left from knuckles would be.

A baseball?

Or was there some type of water toy with which the pathologist was unfamiliar and by which a small boy might be bruised?

He did not yet have children, and it had been many years since he'd spent any time in a pool.

If the child had lived, those bruises would have turned from their light violet shade (lavender?) to a livid purple, and then to yellow, then to deep red, then to a dark purple, before healing. However, these were fresh bruises, and since no blood now circulated in the body, they would never change color or heal.

The funeral parlor cosmetician would have to spackle the one on the boy's neck, perhaps, with some heavy stage makeup—unless the boy was buried in a buttoned-up shirt, perhaps wearing a necktie.

The pathologist assumed there would be an open casket. A drowning victim was often one of the most beautiful of dead bodies—no need for a wig, or to reshape a crushed skull, and no attempt necessary to hide signs of violence or the evidence of the ravages of terminal illnesses. The gray-blue tint of his skin would shift to a rosy glow after embalming.

Luckily, he had not gone unnoticed in the water long enough to display maceration—what was called "washerwoman's skin" because of the wrinkling—and the water had apparently not been particularly cold.

Nothing could look more pristine than this boy's body.

Still, the bruises confused the pathologist—how round they were, a pair, identical in size and shape.

Were these birthmarks?

Of course not.

Before he folded the broken ribcage back over the drained lungs and began to sew the two halves of the torso together again, he placed the small, sharp tip of his scalpel to the bruise on the boy's torso.

The vessels under the skin were ruptured. It took no more than the slightest prick for blood to leak out of the typical contusion and onto the boy's pale and hairless flesh.

This, he recognized, was certainly the result of a very recent injury, or a fall, or a blow. However, since the body would be drained very soon, there could be no way to gauge the seriousness of the injury by observing whether it became spongy and rubbery—a hematoma—or turned into a stiff, firm lump, which might indicate that the blows had occurred postmortem, perhaps after the body was in the ambulance, or earlier, while it was being hauled up from the bottom of the pool.

He chose not to note the bruises on the boy's chart.

It was 100 percent certain that this boy had drowned.

To note the bruises might flag the attention of law enforcement, who might then want to investigate the parents for child abuse, and this was not an abused or neglected child.

His teeth were clean.

His eyes were clear and bright.

He was so healthy that even the capillaries around his nose and in the whites of his eyes hadn't reddened from the strain of suffocation.

The pathologist noticed a slightly pink tinge to those eye whites at first, but quickly he realized this pink was due to the naked eye's exposure to chlorine—that the boy had opened his eyes underwater and wasn't wearing goggles.

The pathologist put a drop of Visine in each eye and watched the pink fade to white, and then wiped away the tears draining out of the corners of the boy's eyes with a cotton swab.

This was a well-fed, clean, cared-for child.

This wasn't a child who'd suffered broken bones, cigarette burns, malnutrition. Even after a day spent in the pool and an evening in the morgue, his curly dark hair smelled clean.

The pathologist pushed the boy's ribcage together again—which was so easy to do with a body as small as this, no more difficult than closing a large dictionary or an oversized Bible—and he took the needle and thread out of the drawer.

One of the reasons he'd become a pathologist instead of a surgeon was because he didn't have the best hand-eye coordination and often his stitches turned out ragged and uneven, like a child's sewing project, and would have left (if he hadn't been practicing on corpses) a living human being perhaps somewhat disfigured.

Still, he did his best.

8

A few months after her son's funeral, Marie Manning knocked on the front door of the house in which the lifeguard lived with her mother. She would not have recognized the woman who came to the door except that her daughter (whose every photograph in the newspaper Marie had memorized by then, desperate to see that girl from every possible angle, from the most microscopic face in the third row of the West Mission Hills choir to a prom photo in which she wore a white eyelet granny dress with a wreath of daisies in her hair) looked exactly like her.

The lifeguard's mother had heard a car door slam in their driveway, looked out, and recognized Marie Manning as the woman who was walking in the direction of their door, wearing house slippers and what appeared to be a man's shirt, too large for her, over a pair of black satiny pajama pants. She'd called out to her daughter to stay upstairs.

Marie Manning tried to yank the screen door open, but the lifeguard's mother had latched it.

But Marie pulled on it until she tore the handle, stumbled backward, and sat down with her face in her hands on one of the paving stones that led up to the front door.

"Mrs. Manning," the lifeguard's mother said from the other side of the screen door, which was now hanging open, broken, in a breeze. "Are you—?"

"You bitch!" Marie Manning screamed. The sun lit up a spray of spit with each word. "You pretty little stupid bitch! You fucking stupid irresponsible bitch! You sat up there showing off your legs, twirling your silver whistle, flipping your ponytail around *while you just let my baby drown*!"

The lifeguard's mother felt her daughter behind her then and turned around to push her gently away from the door.

9

After the drowning, and after all that came after the drowning, Patricia Friedlander seemed to lose the ability to sleep. She could close her eyes and lie down, but all night long she felt every minute as it ticked by her. She felt surprised now and then by how quickly the sun came up some mornings, which was a kind of waking, but she couldn't have been asleep or she could not have remembered so clearly every one of those slow and dark minutes as they passed.

She had no nightmares, no dreams, however.

And during the days—while answering letters, paying bills, buying groceries—Patricia Friedlander almost never thought about Richie Manning, and if she did (surprised to see that Mr.

Manning was driving a new car past her house on the way to work—painted gold, a convertible—or to see Marie coming home with a bag of groceries and her remaining son), she did not think of him as she'd most recently seen him, which had been either at the bottom of the Jolly Rogers pool or in a casket that was too large for him in front of an altar.

When Patricia Friedlander pictured the drowned son of her neighbors, she pictured him still standing in the tunnel between the parking lot and the pool. Wearing orange swimming trunks. Glancing anxiously toward the bright blue beyond the tunnel.

He'd looked somewhat impatient. He'd tugged on his mother's hand.

Thank goodness, Mrs. Friedlander thought to herself, she'd managed to see those three Mannings in that tunnel in time to stop them to talk that day.

Of course, she couldn't have known then that she would never talk to Richie Manning alive again, but it proved to Patricia Friedlander, once more, how precious every minute is, and what a mistake it is to waste any opportunity in this busy life to slow time down for a sweet little chat with a child and his mother. You simply could not know what you were wasting when you wasted such a chance. Sometimes the difference between the last chance and a wasted chance was only a matter of a few accidental seconds.

10

I packed up what most of what I'd brought to New Hampshire with me, but I left behind the things I'd bought while there—the bedspread, dishes, coffee cups, the curtains, and a tablecloth. I stuffed other things (the baby-sized socks Wolfie brought home the day I found out I was pregnant, the crocheted blanket his mother had sent after receiving our good news), along with the hiking boots I wouldn't need again and a New Hampshire sweatshirt that said *Live Free or Die*, into a box, which I left in the apartment complex parking lot, hoping someone who might need such things would find them.

Six

10

Richie stood at the chain-link fence, on the grassy side of it, while he waited for Adult Swim to end.

He waited forever.

While he waited, Richie pressed his face into the dusty steel of the fence.

He moved around until he managed to fit his two eyes into two side-by-side diamonds perfectly.

Then, he could see everything.

He saw Mrs. Friedlander's yellow flowers bobbing up and down as she swam back and forth.

He saw the slide.

Water poured down it.

He saw the lifeguard's seat.

It was empty.

No lifeguard needed to watch Adult Swim.

He saw a man who looked like he was made of leather flex his muscles after he used the railing in the deep end to climb out of the pool. He saw two mothers sitting at the edge of the pool, dangling their feet up to their ankles in the water.

He saw the water. The blue of it. He saw the sun turn the water's surface to shining wrinkles. He saw the black lines painted on the bottom of the pool writhe like giant snakes. He saw everything through those two diamond holes as he waited for Adult Swim to end, forever.

And he could smell the dusty metal of the fence.

He wanted to taste that metal.

Then he put out his tongue.

He liked the taste—warm and rough and sweet and also sour. It tasted like a pen he'd once put in his mouth, which was the taste of being a grown man like his father with an office and a desk with a cup full of pens. It had been his father's pen.

No!

It tasted like the lifeguard's silver whistle when she held it between her lips and blew her breath into it! It tasted exactly the way that whistle tore everything to pieces when it screamed. Turned the sky to confetti! Richie licked at the fence and forgot that all the other children waiting for Adult Swim to end were also standing at the fence until he heard a girl behind him shriek, "Gross! That kid's licking the fence!"

Richie jumped back and looked around.

The red-haired girl!

She was pointing at him!

And now the other children were looking at Richie, making faces, and he felt all the skin on his body that wasn't covered by his orange swim trunks start to prickle. He hurried back to where his mother was sitting at the edge of her lounge chair, bouncing Alex on her knee.

"What's wrong now, Richie?" she asked, but not like she wanted to know.

"Nothing," he said before he sat down hard on his bottom in the grass near her bare feet and crossed his legs.

His mother looked down at him, but she did not look very happy to have him return from the fence to her.

"Please," she said. "Please just try to be patient, Richie."

9

When, in September, the lifeguard returned to West Mission High to begin the first day of her senior year, after skipping the pep rally for the Class of 1970 and arriving to her first class before anyone else was there, she almost couldn't cross the threshold after seeing, beyond it, all the shining desks and the clean windows and the chalkboard on which Mr. Campion had written in yellow chalk in all capital letters:

WELCOME BACK.

On the wall, he'd taped some literature posters—bearded men looking soulfully out of the past and a woman reading from an open book in her hands and another woman with her hair pulled back in a painful-looking bun along with a series of banners under their faces—some inspirational quotes:

"You think your pain and your heartbreak are unprecedented in the history of the world, but then you read." James Baldwin

"Every detail should be an omen and a cause." Jorge Luis Borges

The lifeguard read these while frozen in the doorway.

Surely, he could not have chosen these quotes to write on the board for her?

The lifeguard could not have known this, but Mr. Campion had taped her name to several different desks before rethinking the placement—who would sit next to her, behind her, in front of her?

He'd worked hard to recall the kindest girls, the quietest boys, and which ones, if the lifeguard glanced at them, were most likely to smile at her.

He suspected she'd feel most comfortable near the back of the room, but he also didn't want her to think he'd put her there to separate her from the others. However, she couldn't be in the front, feeling all those eyes behind her. And she couldn't be at the center of the classroom.

Hers had to be the most unremarkable of placements.

So Mr. Campion settled on the third row from the front, the second row from the wall, not too close to his own desk but close enough to the door that she'd know she could escape if she felt the need to do so.

He'd had her in two previous classes, in which he recalled she'd excelled, although he hadn't gotten to know her very well. She wasn't one of the friendlier students, the ones who'd ask questions or hang around after class. It was not until he began to read about her, at the same time everyone else did (every day in the local paper from July through the rest of the summer), that he remembered she'd been his student. He'd known nothing about her then, and now he knew everything.

He knew, for example, that she hadn't attended the funeral. And he'd been furious at the reporter who'd felt the need to publish that information on the front page of the paper.

Of course she hadn't attended the funeral.

What would they have said about her if she had?

What she wore. Whether she wept.

Her mother's attendance was noted under a photograph of "the lifeguard's mother"—a woman who looked like a melted version of her daughter: the same face, but aged, collapsed, deflated—wearing a black dress, twisting a handkerchief between her hands, wearing the expression of someone who'd just stumbled, seasick, off a ship that had been out to sea, riding rough waves for a long time.

Then the pep rally was over, students returned to the hallways, and suddenly the lifeguard was blocking the door as her classmates began to inch around her to get into English. Some of them had blue and gold ribbons in their hair and *West Mission Class of 1970!!* buttons pinned to their shirts and blouses. They smelled like the gymnasium from which they'd just come (varnish, canvas, rubber soles). Luckily there was enough room for them to get past her without pushing. No one told her to get out of the way. No one asked her why she was standing there.

Instead, they acted as if they simply could not see her.

Perhaps, she thought, they couldn't.

Perhaps she wasn't there.

The lifeguard had already forgotten having been dropped off at the school's entrance by her mother and how, before opening the car door and stepping out of it, her mother had leaned over and given her a too-tight hug.

The lifeguard barely remembered walking into the school, looking around the cafeteria, which had a WELCOME BACK TO WMHS banner strung between two posts. She'd squinted at the schedule the secretary handed her, seeing the names of her classes on it—their locations, and the number of her locker, and the six digits of her locker combination, and her schedule:

First Hour Honors English / Campion / Rm 211.

From somewhere at the center of the school she could hear the pep rally: stomping, clapping, chanting.

And then that was over, and she was standing in the doorway to that classroom.

8

Richard Manning looked through his window, down on what might have been the Appalachians if they'd managed to slide themselves a few hundred miles west of where they used to be, as his boy began to drown between the deep end and the shallow end of the Jolly Rogers Swim Club pool.

After the swim meet, they forgot to return the rope to its place at the center of the pool, its two ends attached to two metal hooks.

It was a thick, waxy, rough braid of shredded and compacted polypropylene that was kept afloat by three red buoys—or blue, depending on who you asked and what they remembered.

That rope was meant to separate the shallow end of the pool from the deep end, where not only did the pool get deeper, but the water dropped several degrees and the blue of it darkened.

There, the cement basin sloped down until the bottom of the pool was so far below the surface of the water that swimmers passing over it didn't even cast a shadow on the cement.

Looking down through that clear sky at the impossible barrier of green frothing between himself and his window seat, Richard thought of how much higher above him those astronauts were. He'd missed the launch with his son but would be home in time to watch the landing.

In the briefcase (a shiny, new black leather case, very sleek, which Marie had picked out for him when he got his promotion last April, now stowed beneath the seat in front of him), Richard had the folders he needed, and all the necessary paperwork, and few nice pens they would pass around the oak or cherry or mahogany table to sign, if all went well. He also had a silk scarf with triangles on it for Marie, wrapped in tissue. The previous afternoon, between a meeting and the meeting after it, he'd asked the girl behind the desk at his hotel what he should do in Atlanta with a few hours to kill, and she'd suggested he walk down to the viaduct and see a sculpture that had just been finished, *Atlanta from the Ashes.*

Despite the heat and humidity, Richard had walked to it, but he hadn't found the sculpture particularly interesting. With the sun beating down on it, the bronze woman was hard to look at without being blinded. The woman had her arms lifted above her head and the talons of a phoenix were in her hands. He assumed that she was supposed to be sending the bird up into the sky, out of the ashes, but to Richard it looked like she could just as easily be tugging it out of the air, back down to her, on Earth.

He needed to bring presents home with him and might not have time to shop in Dallas, so he turned away from the statue and looked around until he saw the department store that had commissioned it and the OPEN sign on the door, and since the doors were closed, he knew there'd be air-conditioning, so he headed there, where he bought the scarf for Marie.

He'd felt self-conscious at the scarf counter, with so many women standing around him, asking to look at different scarves, fingering the material, holding scarves to their necks and looking at themselves in one of the round mirrors set out for that purpose on the display case.

When a girl behind the counter—nice looking but trying too hard, maybe: her cheeks too rouged, her cat-eye glasses too cute, her hair stiff with spray—asked if she could help him, Richard pointed at a polka-dotted one. The girl wrapped it in tissue and put it in a slender box for him, took his money, gave him his change. But before he left the store and its air-conditioning to walk back to his hotel, Richard opened the box to look at it again, hoping he'd chosen something his wife would like.

But there were no polka dots on this scarf.

The design was geometric, no circles at all. All sharp edges. Triangles, rectangles, squares. Lime green and pale orange, scattered.

Had he already forgotten the scarf he'd chosen, or had the girl given him the wrong scarf?

Marie wouldn't like it, he thought. It wasn't soft enough. It was decorated like one of the cocktail napkins at the Comet Club where he used to bowl and made him think of something the astronauts' wives would wear—not today (all of them dressed very formally, with identical floral stoles around their shoulders, gazing happily at their husbands, who smiled happily back out at them from inside their little triangle, as if everybody was going to meet up again in a couple of hours at the beach), but might be wearing in one of those photo spreads in *Life:*

Astronauts at home, sitting on deck chairs while their wives stood behind them.

He'd seen plenty of those wives in the last few weeks. Everyone had. It always left Richard feeling satisfied, seeing those women, who were not—even Buzz Aldrin's wife, the best-looking one—exactly knock-outs. Attractive enough, but Marie could have outshone any one of them. And, to think, those astronauts could've had any women on Earth they wanted, but somehow Richard had ended up with the most beautiful of the four wives.

Of course, Marie would never have married an astronaut.

Marie would start to pace and wring her hands, her eyes filling up with tears when Richard simply talked about making the shift from Steelcase to AmeriWay.

And, frankly, Richard was not quite sure he would enjoy being married to a woman that independent anyway.

A woman like that would not be lying awake tonight, waiting for him to get home, no matter how late it got.

If he was married to a wife like Buzz Aldrin's, she would probably be fast asleep or reading a book.

What Richard had done was marry the nicest girl he'd ever met, who hadn't been going to his university, but whom he assumed at the time was taking classes there because she worked in his dormitory cafeteria, a job mostly done by students—but also, as it turned out, sometimes by teens who lived in town.

Marie Pulaski must've shyly scooped up his mashed potatoes and left a neat little moon-shaped pile of them for him on his plate twenty times before he got up the courage to ask her name.

They must have gone on a dozen dates before he felt sure she wouldn't scream and run if he tried to hold her hand.

But within a few days of their first kiss, he'd already asked her to marry him, even though they both knew they needed to wait at least a year and a half, until he'd finished his degree and she was eighteen.

He was plain lucky to have married the nicest girl he ever met, even if she didn't share his ambitions for their family, for their prosperity.

Well, he wasn't any Neil Armstrong, either.

He wasn't going to be walking on the moon or needing the kind of wife who could smile and wave goodbye to him before he was launched into space.

Still, he could've used a bit of a boost now and then, the sense that she had some confidence in him, that she could imagine him taking a risk and not failing, that instead of ruining their lives by taking some chances he might be able to improve their lives.

He hoped Marie would like the scarf. He wouldn't tell her that it was a salesgirl's mistake.

Also in his briefcase, for Alex, Richard had a small rubber ax, which had been a lucky find at the airport gift shop, since Alex had recently become interested in a lumberjack he'd seen in a cartoon and had been going around the house pretending to be chopping down the chair legs and the legs of the coffee table.

For Richie he'd bought a yo-yo. A Deluxe Edition Duncan.

It was a deep ruby red. It was so red that it was almost black.

It would have been the first yo-yo Richie ever owned.

His father would have taught him how to release it with the spring and then snap it back.

And after Richie got the hang of that, Richard would have taught him the few tricks he remembered from his own childhood—Walk the Dog, the Pin Wheel, Man on the Flying Trapeze—after which Richie would learn his own tricks, teaching them to himself or learning them from his friends during recess next fall at West Mission Elementary School, where, instead of a desk with his name on it in his first-grade classroom, there would be a cherry tree planted outside the classroom window, at the base of which there would be a small brass plaque: *This tree is planted in memory of Richie Manning: August 1963–July 16, 1969.*

But eventually his son would have gotten better and better with the yo-yo, better than Richard himself had ever been as a boy, and the tricks Richie would learn on the playground and invent for himself through experimentation—trying and failing, practicing over and over again until he mastered them—his son would eventually have taught to his father.

7

Wonder Bread.

Marie took one of the sandwiches—so weightless it might have floated from her hand if she'd let go—out of the picnic basket to examine it.

Insubstantial as the future or memory, Wonder Bread didn't even seem like *food.*

Or it seemed like food for ghosts, or angels, or for the kind of fairytale creatures from that needed no nutrition to live, for whom actual food might be a hindrance to their floating through the air on their transparent wings.

But she made lunch out of it for her growing boy anyway—this bread she wouldn't even have bothered to feed to swans down by the pond behind the AmeriWay complex Richard liked to take them to for picnics. She feared that bread might ball up and get stuck in their slender throats and choke them.

Marie had never intended to feed such things to her children, either. Wonder Bread. Pop Tarts. She'd planned to make the heavy dark breads her mother used to bake, which were hard to chew but with ingredients that seemed to come from Earth instead of out of the ether. But what could she do? The commercials with their cartoons—tigers, leprechauns, rabbits—played every fifteen minutes during cartoon time on Saturday mornings, and Richie was only two and a half when he first lunged out of the cart at the supermarket to grab for a cereal box with Tony the Tiger on it that he recognized from TV.

After that, there was no going back.

There was Tang in the sippy cup (after all, it had been invented for astronauts!), and then the Kool-Aid (no excuse for that), and then the Oreos, after which Marie's oatmeal cookies were left to molder in the cookie jar, untouched, unless the Oreos had all been eaten.

Another mother, a stronger mother, might have been able to stand between her son and his demands and feed him spinach instead of Jell-O with his hot dogs. But she was not that mother. It wasn't that she couldn't bear the whining or the nagging, but it was perhaps because it was all still so close to the surface for her—her own childhood, which hadn't been impoverished, exactly, but she had never forgotten all the things she'd wanted as a child, intensely, like the penny loafers and the doll-sized baby carriage, and the weight of *no* like an anchor being dropped onto her child-sized chest.

And maybe the extra vitamins they put in the food made a difference after all.

The boys looked healthy and well-fed.

Alex was still mostly baby fat, chubby cheeks. Richie was skinny, but he was pure-muscle skinny. His whole body was one long muscle. At the swim club she'd watch him pull himself up out of the water, and his body reminded her of a fish, and how a fish is just one slap of flesh: that insistent force of a fish pulled out of Crystal Lake at the end of her father's fishing line, and how it struggled to get out of its body when he tossed it onto the faded wood of a fishing pier.

Those fish looked as if their lives had been poured into very flexible, sequined bags, and then had been struck by lightning.

Richie was growing so fast!

In the fall, before starting first grade, he was going to need all new clothes. His legs were so much longer already than they had been in April that the black pants that went with the suit they'd bought him to wear to his aunt's wedding (ring bearer) in May were already an inch above his ankles.

She filled the thermos with Tang from the pitcher in the fridge.

She placed three apples carefully at the bottom of the picnic basket.

She'd bring a couple dollars with her, too, to buy them popsicles from the snack bar if they wanted them, although she'd promised Richard she wouldn't waste money on snacks. ("Chum Rogers is already minting his own money with that pool, and then to be selling us potato chips at the price of gold doubloons on top of our membership dues . . .") But sometimes it was the only way she could convince Richie to get out of the pool, to dry off, to get ready to head back home to take a bath, eat dinner—*a popsicle if you don't give me any trouble.*

"Mama?"

Marie was startled to hear Richie's voice, to find him standing in the threshold.

She'd thought he was still in the living room with his brother, watching whatever was left of the excitement of the astronauts, the rocket launch, on the television.

"Are we ever going to the pool?"

6

She had become a lifeguard at the Jolly Rogers Swim Club when she turned sixteen not only because she had the swimming skills and the Red Cross certificate needed for the job and she needed to save money for college, but because she loved children.

When she was little, the lifeguard would beg her mother incessantly to have a second child so that she could have a little sister or a brother. She imagined that the sibling would be her own baby. She would change its diaper, rock it to sleep, feed it with a bottle when it was hungry. She would give it pet names. Sissy or Buzzard or Baby.

Only later would she realize how painful this request might have been for her mother, who'd tried and failed for so long to conceive even one child. There would never be a second, so the lifeguard babysat for families all over the neighborhood, instead of her siblings.

She loved those children.

When they finally fell asleep at night, the lifeguard would go into their rooms and stand beside their beds. She would bring a cup of water with her. She would dip two fingers in the cup, lean down, and draw a cross with the water on their foreheads.

In the name of the Father . . .

She didn't know whether or not most of them had been baptized already, but it didn't matter unless they hadn't been.

If they hadn't been and died, they would be left at the gate to heaven.

Which didn't seem fair to the lifeguard, but which she believed anyway, and so she baptized them, and when she became a lifeguard.

She'd practiced bringing the drowned back to life in the basement of the Mission Hills Recreation Center every Friday night for ten weeks before she received her certificate, kneeling on the linoleum, bent over the rubber torso of Rescue Annie—that teen-girl-sized doll who bore the face of a girl who'd drowned in the Seine in 1880. She never managed to bring that doll to life, but she was praised for her skill by the Red Cross instructor, and she carried a laminated card with a red cross and her name on it in her wallet.

Just as the lifeguard had predicted, the boy on his way to the slide started, after a few faster and longer strides proved too slow for him, to run.

When she brought the whistle to her lips and blew it, he stopped and looked up at her.

"Hey, buddy," she called down. "No running. Okay? Remember?"

The boy's eyes widened. His face had already been red—from sunburn, perhaps, and from the cold water and from excitement and exertion—but he seemed to flush more deeply then. Their eyes met. She smiled down at him.

5

The night before the moon launch, while Richard was away on his business trip, the boys slept in their fire-retardant pajamas, while Marie lay awake across the hall from them in the half empty bed, staring at the ceiling, wondering why she felt so ill at ease.

Everything was fine.

Why must she be filled with such dread?

When she'd finally gotten the boys into bed, she'd turned the television on, thinking she would watch the news, and sat down on the couch.

But she was exhausted.

She went to the bedroom and changed into a white nightgown

and got in bed and had drifted in and out of sleep before she found herself wide awake again.

Had she forgotten to turn the television off downstairs?

She thought she could hear, below her, men's voices.

In Kazakhstan, the Soviets were testing a nuclear device and, although the radiation was invisible, it would settle on the backs of a herd of reindeer, which would then move silently across the continent.

Also, Björn Borg had just won the 93rd Men's Wimbledon Tennis Championship, and now he was drunk. Instead of the joy he knew he should have felt, Borg felt shame. At the bar that night, he told all the beautiful women around him, for the four millionth time, about how, as a four-year-old, he'd become obsessed with a small golden tennis racket his father had won in a ping-pong tournament, and how he'd begged for it until finally his father had given it to him—

"And this was the beginning of my life. A Swedish fairytale!"

Was it his imagination or did they look at him as if they thought he was pig, a tyrant, the way his mother used to look at his father?

Marie rolled onto her back in bed and became aware, if only vaguely, that the planet was revolving.

It was, of course, revolving very slowly, so that the next day was still thousands and thousands of miles and many hours away, but she could feel it heading in her direction:

Tomorrow would come, as it always did, and everything would be the same as it had been today, which meant that everything would be fine. She would take the boys to the pool. It was going to be sunny. And by the time they got back to the house, Richard would be home from his business trip. If, by then, she still felt so anxious, she could take one of those Valiums her friend Bette had given to her. ("My kids are ten and twelve now. You need these more than I do, honey.") She'd so far only taken one, once, after her mother's funeral. She'd swallowed it with a Dixie cup of skim milk and had then fallen asleep in her funeral dress on top of the bedspread. No dreams. She woke up thinking she'd been awake.

Or, after dinner, she could ask Rich to take the boys to the park, and maybe she could just relax in the bathtub, in cool water (not hot), without waiting, as she did when the boys were in the house, for a knock on the door and, *Mama, Alex just threw up* . . .

Yes, it was the deep dark blue of a summer night by then, and the sun had completely set, but that just meant it was shining somewhere else, she knew.

The neighborhood was quiet.

The windows were open, but she couldn't hear even a cricket.

Not even one dog barked anywhere.

Everything was fine.

Marie Manning willed herself to close her eyes again, but the longer she stared at the ceiling, the more it felt as if the ceiling were her eyelids.

And the silence didn't calm her the way it should have, either.

It was like the indifferent silence of outer space—an indifference that, actually, Marie took great comfort in some nights, that sense that nothing mattered, because nothing would ever change—but tonight she didn't.

Still, if there was nothing wrong, wasn't everything exactly as it was supposed to be?

Some night in the future she'd lie in bed and remember this night and think how easy it is to see the past from the future. How much closer everything appears when it's behind you.

4

A few days later, instead of driving their children to a party for some kindergarten boy's sixth birthday in someone's backyard, the parents of Richie's kindergarten playmates would drive (some with and some without their own children) to his funeral.

That day, too, would be sunny, with a sky so cloudless it looked like the briefest stab with the tip of a sharp knife could puncture it, and then that hazy film would split wide open and all the darkness behind it would spill onto them, along with everything else up there—the sun along with all the other stars, and the planets, as well as the moon (their own moon and also the moons of the other planets). It would crush them and burn them, just as they were stepping out of their cars, onto the sticky tar of the church parking lot, before they'd even had time to climb the steps to the open doors of Trinity Lutheran Church, where the altar was drowning in flowers and, behind the altar, an enormous Christ writhed in German agony nailed to a cross that was nailed to a wall.

But nothing fell out of the sky onto the funeral goers. They entered the church, blind and blinking until their eyes had time to adjust to the darkness that followed all the brilliance that was still bouncing off the chrome and glass of their cars in the church parking lot behind them.

All those flowers mixed with women's perfume, along with the scent of candlewax melting and the humidity of human breath, perspiration, as well as, perhaps, the smell of coffee that was being brewed in the church basement, where it would be waiting for them when the service ended.

Outside, there were still some drivers behind the wheels of their cars, circling, searching for parking spots, listening to the urgent updates about the astronauts on their radios, until it became too much tragedy at once, listening to these updates while circling a church parking lot in order to attend a kindergartner's funeral, and they parked down the block.

As it turned out, they were the lucky ones. Having to walk farther to the church, they arrived too late, behind too many others still entering the open doors and never heard Marie Manning's keening—so urgent and cadenced and growing louder and more strident that several of them (especially those who'd been at the swim club when the boy had drowned) briefly wondered if another ambulance might be zigzagging through traffic, running through stoplights, speeding its way toward them.

The boy's mother was reaching into her son's coffin as she wailed.

Was she trying to lift him out of it?

The boy's father stood and hurried toward her, but then, still a few feet away from her and his son, he froze.

Most of them had closed or covered their eyes before a larger man, in dress blues, took the child from her, returned him to his too-large casket (why had a child's size not been made?) and then returned to Marie and put his hands on her shoulders and tried to look into her eyes. She struggled away from him until he was able to wrap his arms around her torso, lift her off her feet, and carry her away from the front of the church as she screamed, "That bitch killed my baby! That stupid little slut let my son drown!"

Then, from somewhere behind the altar, a door was heard to slam.

Either the boy's mother had been taken to some sound-proofed room, or she'd passed out. Or maybe the Marine—who was, it was whispered, Mrs. Manning's brother, home from Vietnam because of his nephew's death—had put his hand over her mouth, or someone else had been waiting there with a syringe to tranquilize her.

A few of those sitting in pews close to the exits slipped out of the church, back into the parking lot. Some sobbed softly where they sat. While the others, who'd had to park on the grass, were still trapped in the crowd at the entrance, too many at once to push through the church doors.

But those in the front of the church saw Richard Manning lean over the coffin to readjust his son's miniature clip-on tie (red, which was probably his favorite color) while an elderly church lady picked up the white satin pillow that had fallen to the floor from the coffin and stuffed it clumsily behind the boy's head, while the organist swept down the aisle in his choir robe, sat down at his bench, hunched over the keyboard, and began to play "O Savior, Precious Savior," a hymn that many of them had greatly enjoyed singing on Easter Sundays (*we worship you, we bless you, to you alone we sing*), but which they would never want to hear, let alone sing, ever again.

3

One of the secretaries whispered to another, after Richard Manning passed them at the front desk on the way to his office, bestowing his *good mornings* on them, dressed in one of his many sharp, dark suits and with a blue silk tie around his neck and closed his office door behind him, "They say he sold his soul, you know . . ."

The secretary's name was Linda, and she'd been working in that office, at that desk, for a decade, was the mother of four grown women, but she was still called the Main Office Girl.

The Assistant Office Girl beside her was not yet twenty. Her name was Theresa. She wore an engagement ring that was too large for her—a tiny diamond held by prongs to a thin gold band—which slid up and down her finger as she took dictation or typed.

"What do you mean?" Theresa asked

"You don't know? His boy, three years ago. The tragedy? Didn't you read about it? Richie Manning? Five years old?"

"No," Theresa said. "I thought he said his son just started kindergarten."

"No, no. That's *Alex,* the younger son. Richie Manning drowned."

"Oh God."

Linda took a breath, exhaled it, and went on, "Richie Manning at a swim club." She nodded toward Richard Manning's closed door, and at the brass plaque that his name had been engraved on a few summers ago.

"Oh God," Theresa said again.

Theresa liked Mr. Manning, but deep down, she didn't care about his life. She just needed this job for a few more months. After she and Greg got married, they were going to start a family right away, and Theresa would quit her job.

A cold and artificial breeze began at Theresa's ankles, crept up her pantyhose. It was probably just the air-conditioning kicking in, but it felt different. It felt like a memory and a premonition making their way together from her toes to her brain.

"Yes." Linda nodded. "Then the next week, George Stewart died." This time she pointed at Mr. Manning's door while also nodding at it again. "And suddenly we had a new brass plaque and a new sales director. Richard Manning. Fancy that. The man started working for AmeriWay within two weeks of burying his boy, and then he made a million dollars in less than six months. The Big Boss threw a big party at the Pantlind, rented out the whole place, even the janitors were invited—open bar, glittery dollar sign decorations dangling from the ceiling, and he presented Richard Manning with that gold watch he's always wearing. Then the Mannings moved out of their little bungalow into the Brody Mansion."

"The Brody Mansion? Oh God."

Theresa hadn't grown up in Mission Hills, but everyone knew about the Brody Mansion. Its ballroom and theater. Its fountain. How it sprawled across almost an entire block of West Mission Hills.

Theresa swallowed, closed her eyes for a moment, thinking back, opened her eyes and looked over at Linda and said, "So, you're telling me that Richard Manning got rich in exchange for his son drowning at a swim club?"

Theresa wanted to sound as disapproving of Linda's mean-spirited gossip as she could, but she saw by the satisfied look on Linda's face that her question had been interpreted as one of astonished sincerity instead.

Linda shrugged. "Well, you can't have everything in this life. Have you ever seen his wife?"

"I don't think so," Theresa said.

"Well, you'll know who she is when you see her. Dark hair. Sunglasses. Always wearing a little shift and high heels. She looks like a movie star. But just wait until she takes off those sunglasses . . ."

"Why?"

"Because there's *nothing there*."

Linda had turned her desk chair all the way around to stare straight into Theresa's eyes, as if waiting for a response, but Theresa just looked away, down to her finger and the little diamond held up by four golden prongs. She slid the band (too loose) up over her knuckle, pushed it back down again. When she looked up again, Linda was still staring.

"Why are you telling me this?" Theresa asked her.

Linda shrugged.

She wore a sleeveless blouse under a crocheted sweater, and through the holes in her sweater Theresa could see that the flesh on the older woman's arms was spotted.

"Isn't Greg with AmeriWay now?" Linda asked, as if she were changing the subject, before she turned back to her own desk.

"Yes," Theresa said. "Why?"

Her fiancé had just started working for AmeriWay a few weeks earlier, and the Big Boss had already proclaimed him to be "an up-and-comer, our next sensational success!"

"Just happy for you," Linda said.

Theresa went back to her own desk, took a sheet of paper out of her inbox and tried to read it, but she could only look at the words without understanding them. She took a pen out of her top drawer. She put the pen down and began to slide her engagement ring around on her finger again. Finally, she felt angry. She turned around and said to Linda, "I wish you hadn't told me any of this. It's just horrible to say that these people brought something like that tragedy on themselves. *On purpose.*"

"Well, I'm not the one who said it. I'm just telling you what is said." Linda took a letter opener that was shaped and engraved like a miniature sword to rip open an envelope in one clean swipe. "Don't blame the messenger."

"Well, no one should say such things. About anyone. Ever."

Linda stopped then and swiveled again in her chair. She narrowed her eyes at Theresa and, still holding the letter opener, she said, "How dare you tell me what I—"

She'd intended to say more—more about fortune and misfortune, blessings and punishments, the dangers of Satan, about which she knew far more than this Assistant Girl with her cheap engagement ring—but just then Mr. Manning opened his office door carrying a folder, biting an expensive pen between his teeth, headed for a meeting of other big shots like himself.

2

The funeral organist had either been playing very quietly (despite the massive pipes that rose up behind his back as he sat at his instrument) or had stopped playing when the mother left her pew to go to her son.

This was no European cathedral, but for a Lutheran church founded by Germans a century earlier in a mid-sized Midwestern town, it was a fairly large, high-ceilinged—a dignified structure. From the outside it looked mostly like bricks and aluminum, but inside there was an enormous, emaciated Jesus with a crown of thorns on his head nailed to a wall behind the altar, a gift from their sister church—which, like Dachau, was just outside of Munich—and there were stained glass windows pouring bits and pieces of brilliance onto the parishioners, especially on a day like this, another perfectly sunny day in a string of perfectly sunny summer days—and the altar was draped with linen and lace and flowers and goblets and silver crosses and melting candles with arrowlike flames in front of which Richie Manning's kindergarten picture smiled—silly, displaying a missing tooth with a fake blue sky behind him, wearing a plaid shirt with the top button closed around his throat so that it looked too tight (which had been the school photographer's suggestion, no one else's).

Behind all this, the pipes of the organ (an instrument that had been donated by one of Mission Hill's most devoted Lutherans and most prosperous AmeriWay employees, and which would one day be featured in a national magazine in an article called "Hidden Gems of the Midwest") bloomed and buzzed.

Richie Manning's feet in their white socks dangled, but his mother held his head up in one hand, kissing and kissing his forehead, before she turned toward the congregation, some of whom were on their knees now, and some of whom were standing, a few of whom had begun to rush toward her, too, and then stopped, not knowing what they would do if they reached her.

No one would recall how long the organist's silence lasted.

1

"Richie!"

"Richie!"

He was twirling in the water, using his arms to turn his body around and around, because he didn't need his feet to stand on, because the water was holding him up, and he was dunking under (like being inside a rock—everything quiet, all alone) and then popping back up to the surface, the sun zapping into his eyes, and all that noise, and a boy dog-paddling toward him, a girl's red hair flashing over the water, and then she was upside down: he could see her feet sticking out of the water. She must've been standing on her hands!

He heard it in some part of him, and recognized his name, his mother's voice, but that part of him went away when he ducked under again. Just a boom that came from inside of him, and a silence hiding him from all sound.

He never knew how he knew when he had to breathe, but he never felt afraid, since his body knew, and then he was breaking through the water into the air again to take a breath, and then he—

"*Richie Manning! RIGHT NOW.*"

And there was no ignoring it then. His whole name. His mother not only saying it, but shouting it, and although he had to turn around and around before he could see her over the arms and feet of the other children in the pool and the children standing at the edge of it, ready to jump in, the third time around, despite feeling dizzy, he did.

His mother was at the edge of the shallow end, just straightening up after having bent over, trying to get his attention, while all the other children around Richie ignored her, the way they all ignored every mother except their own.

He looked up at her. She was frowning. Alex had his fat legs wrapped around her tummy and his butt resting on her hip, and he was laughing, pointing at the beach ball, which, now, two older boys, closer to the deep end, were throwing to each other, faster and harder than Richie could ever have thrown a ball through the air, especially a ball that was filled with air.

These bigger boys, their tricks.

Now and then one of them would get a running start and, instead of going through the gate at the end of Adult Swim, he would leap over the chain-link fence while his friends laughed, and maybe the lifeguard never noticed because her back was to them, but some other mother might say, "Hey!" but even if it was that boy's own mother, he ignored her.

Richie was not like those boys.

He turned and paddled toward his mother.

"Get up here now," she said when he got close enough to hear her, and she pointed at the cement under her feet again.

"Me?" he asked, pretending he didn't know, which wasn't exactly the same as *lying.*

His mother pointed to the edge of the pool where her own feet were.

"Here."

He paddled all the way there and held onto the edge. His mother bent down and said, "You have one minute to get out of this pool to come with me while I take Alex to the potty."

"What? Why?" Richie asked.

But she'd already straightened up and stepped away and didn't answer his question.

She pretended (Richie always know when she was doing it, too) to be walking away as if she didn't care anymore whether he followed her or not, and even though he knew she was pretending, his heart started to beat harder, and he felt tears mixed in with the chlorine start to sting, and used his arms to pull himself up over the cement edge of the pool. He was almost up, but it was slippery, so he kicked his legs behind him to get the water to help push him out. It hurt. That rough edge scraped his stomach.

Superficial epidermal trauma to torso.

"Mommy?"

He watched her legs continue to move in the direction of the potty, where she was taking Alex.

He called out again.

She stopped then, turned around, and said, "What?"

"There's a lifeguard, Mommy," he said. "So why—?"

It was his last chance.

He pointed to the lifeguard in her sunglasses, twirling her whistle.

From up there, she could see them all!

But his mother didn't even glance at the lifeguard. She looked, instead, harder into Richie's eyes, and then she turned her back, hoisted Alex higher on her hip, and Richie hurried to catch up to them.

Seven

1

Becca had never paid any attention to the newspaper before. Her mother had never subscribed to it, but her stepfather did, and every afternoon some boy threw one, rolled up with a red rubber band around it, onto their front steps.

After that little boy drowned, Becca would come into the kitchen in the morning to find, almost every morning for a couple of weeks, the *Mission Hills Herald* on the table in front of her chair. During those weeks, Becca had come to believe that this newspaper, which she'd almost never even seen before they moved into her stepfather's house, was a publication dedicated to drownings and astronauts. Usually, she just moved the paper to the middle of the table after filling her Cheerios bowl and sitting down in her chair. But sometimes she would read.

"We're going to fill the thing with dirt, cover it with cement, and someone can build a gas station or a grocery store on it or use it for a parking lot. But no one will ever drown in that pool again."

Chum Rogers, the man who opened the Jolly Rogers Swim Club, had said that. It was reported that he "broke down" during the interview in which he said it.

There were neighbors quoted in the paper who all said what a good boy the drowned one was, and what a perfect family he'd come from. The principal of West Mission Hills Elementary School said he "couldn't believe it." And a kindergarten teacher named Mrs. Talifero was at the bottom of the front page one day in a photograph, walking out of a church, holding a handkerchief to her face. The newspaper people said that Mrs. Talifero was too upset to speak with them.

Everything about the drowned boy stayed the same from one day to the next.

But the news about the lifeguard kept changing.

At first, it wasn't her fault. It wasn't *anybody's* fault.

Then: LIFEGUARD WAS DISTRACTED, POOL CLUB MEMBERS SAY

Then she flunked her driver's license test by running over an orange cone. Also, once she lost her expensive book and had laughed with some other girls in the choir while they stood on the stage for graduation and when they were supposed to be singing the national anthem.

Becca didn't think those last things sounded bad enough to get into the newspaper, and it worried her because she didn't ever want to have her name or her picture on anyone's table while they ate Cheerios. She especially didn't want to see anyone quoted under her school picture saying, "There was just one person responsible for that boy's drowning—the lifeguard."

Her sister came into the kitchen then. She was the other daughter of Becca's mother, and she was in college already. She was visiting because she felt like sleeping on Becca's floor. ("Not really," she'd said. "I want to sleep in your bed and you have to sleep on the floor.")

Aimee hadn't visited since their mother got married and they moved in with her stepfather—and Davey, and Chrissy.

She'd just gotten home the day after that boy drowned.

"Are you home to go to that boy's funeral?" Becca asked. Her mother had already said that she would be going.

"No," Aimee said. "He's not why I came home."

2

Mr. Campion hurried after the lifeguard, calling her name, but he reached the stairwell just in time to watch her run down it with incredible speed, and then he stopped, knowing he couldn't be seen chasing a student down the stairwell, and also not knowing what he would do if he caught her.

He went back to his classroom, where the students sat in strange silence. "Hi, class," he said, out of breath. It was a warm morning, still like summer, and he could feel a stream of sweat trickle down his back and the sweat under his arms soaking into his shirt.

"Go ahead and talk to each other, just don't get too loud for Mrs. Mitchell next door! I'll be just a minute. I have to call the office."

He turned his back to the class and picked up the receiver of the classroom phone, dialed O for Office and, as quietly as possible, told the secretary when she answered what had happened.

"Oh my God," Cynthia Beck said. Only an hour earlier the two of them had been speculating about how the lifeguard would be received by her classmates, not to mention a number of teachers who knew the Mannings or had simply read the local newspaper articles and decided the boy's drowning had been her fault.

"Someone needs to call her mother," Peter said. "Can you or Jim do that? I have to teach my class."

"Okay, okay, sure, of course," Miss Beck said.

He hung up, turned to the class and said, "Welcome," again and then, "As you may know, I'm Mr. Campion."

3

The lifeguard blew her whistle!

Richie hadn't even seen her walk through the gate, but then, there she was above them, back on her white throne, crossing her legs, blowing into her whistle, pulling the tangy metal of it out of her mouth to take a breath before she shouted: "End of Adult Swim! Free Swim! *No pushing! No running, kids!*"

And then all of them pushed in one running surge. If you were in the front, you were pushed out of the way. If you were in the middle, you were taken along with the others whether or not you wanted to, and if you slowed down you would feel an elbow jabbed into you or a bigger boy's chest bumping hard against your back.

So, instead of slowing down, as the lifeguard shouted at them to do, they moved faster and together like the pledge of *one nation under God, invisible* or what Walter Concrete had said that morning about how the whole of humankind had come together to go to the moon. So, Richie knew, there was nothing to do about it now. Whether you wanted to run or push or go to the moon or not.

And then, suddenly, Richie was standing alone, as the children around him scattered and jumped and dove into the pool, turning the water into splashing foam, and all of it was there—that shifting mirror, that bubbly window into which one child after another smashed—where it had been waiting just for him.

4

I'd packed my car so full that there was only going to be enough room left in it for me to sit at the wheel to drive to Michigan.

"Sure," my sister said when I called, pretending to sound surprised that Wolfie and I had split up and that I was moving home. "You can stay in Jonah's old room, and if you stay sober and help me with our mother you don't have to pay me any rent until you get a job."

"Thank you."

"*Come on,*" she said. "I'm joking! You don't have to do anything except come home."

"Oh," I said, but I was still stinging. It wasn't that I didn't plan to get a job and pay my own expenses, I was just surprised to hear her say it. For two decades by then she'd never suggested I would be capable, ever, of owing her, anything, ever again. We were even. Or that had seemed to me to have been our understanding since the summer of 1969.

"Are you there?"

"Yeah. I'll call you from the road tomorrow."

"Are you drunk?"

"No," I lied.

"Are you sure?"

Yes.

I couldn't say it.

"Don't you dare drive drunk," she said.

"I won't," I said, and believed I wouldn't. I would be sober by tomorrow. It was only noon, today, so I poured what was left of a bottle of Jim Beam into my cup. There was no Diet Coke left in the refrigerator—there was nothing in the refrigerator now—so I drank it straight, in one gulp. I hated whiskey. I held a paper towel to my mouth in case I couldn't keep it down and sat on the floor with my back to the bed. When the phone rang, I let the broken answering machine answer.

5

One night Richard Manning woke up to find his wife Marie beside him in their bed, looking down on him. Her round face was illuminated by a crack of moonlight splitting through the window shade and sill, and he told her the one true thing he knew with any certainty anymore, that the tragedy that had become their lives was entirely her fault.

He got out of bed, turned his back to her, put his fists against the wall, and asked her if she was happy that their son was buried in that cheap piece of shit for a casket?

When she didn't answer, he punched the wall.

The house was made of sawdust. His fist went straight through it. He could tear the thing down that night with his bare hands.

He asked her next if she was she happy that he'd agreed to put off their trip to Yellowstone for a year so they'd have enough money in her Vacation jar and not have to take it out of their savings.

He withdrew his fist in the silence and punched the wall again.

Was she happy that she hadn't let him go to AmeriWay sooner? Because if he'd been working *there* that summer they'd have had a membership to the West Mission Hills Country Club, where there was a children's pool with *no deep end*, and lifeguards who—

He punched the wall and told her that she'd stood in the way of everything he'd ever wanted. "*I hate waste!*"

Waste!

What had she done with their future except *waste* it?!

What had she been *saving* it for?

Was she happy now? Tidy little nest egg and an inexpensive casket!

A *cheap* casket.

Well, she wasn't going to strangle his dreams any longer. He was at least going to have that pink granite stone hauled away and have it replaced with an actual object of art, something like no other child before Richie had ever been buried under.

Waste!

Ha!

He punched a fist through one of the holes he'd already punched and felt the lack of resistance as impotence, as shame. He sat down hard on the floor and pressed his sore knuckles into his eyes.

"Waste."

He laughed.

And he recalled that the faceless hairless man in the basement of the funeral home had said something along these lines, too. "You don't want to waste your money, Mr. Manning. It might be a better use of precious funds to donate them to the hospital, perhaps a corridor of which could be named for your son, or maybe to a public park, a memorial? Or a scholarship could be created in his name. Or maybe some new playground equipment for his elementary school. Or—"

He didn't know if Marie was still in their bed and didn't care.

She wasn't.

6

"Aren't you going to have some breakfast before you leave? A bowl of Cheerios at least? Can I make you a peanut butter sandwich? It's almost lunchtime, and we haven't eaten."

"No, Mom. I'll eat lunch at the pool."

"Be careful driving," her mother said.

The lifeguard took the car keys from her mother and, before putting on her sunglasses, stepped outside.

It was such a bright day.

She couldn't see a thing.

The sun bounced off the chrome and mirrors of her mother's Duster in blinding daggers.

It was hot, getting hotter. There was the smell of something that was decomposing inside the aluminum garbage can next to the garage. Sweet. But rotten. It was going to attract flies, and the flies would get into the kitchen. She would need to remind her mother to put out the flypaper, which her father used to do every year in the middle of summer.

7

Alex had been in the attic many times, but usually in the company of friends who wanted to climb into the cupola above it, not by himself.

It was a space both cramped and cavernous—high ceilings, exposed beams, many little alcoves and concealed corners, but it was so stuffed with boxes and furniture and racks of clothes and baskets full of things like cloth napkins and doilies, half-knitted sweaters, balls of yarn, old copies of *National Geographic* and *Life* magazines—many of which Alex believed must have belonged to the Brodys, or some family that came after them and before his family, since the dates were so old, and these were not magazines he'd ever seen his parents read, nor had he ever seen his mother knit a sweater or buy a ball of yarn.

And there was so much up there! Christmas decorations he'd never seen—little felt elves, a paper cut-out of a snowman, a wreath with shriveled slices of orange stuck all over it. Once, while looking for the snorkel gear his father had bought him during their vacation in Costa Rica, which he'd decided would be fun to try in Crystal Lake, he came upon a red plastic sled covered in a blue blanket. It wasn't a sled he'd ever seen. It was not his own sled, which had been a Garton Silver Streak with steel runners.

These were strangers' possessions. His own family could not possibly have accumulated so much before they moved into the Brody Mansion, and since then he remembered receiving no gifts of plastic trucks or rocket ships. If any of these toys had been his at one time, he'd long since forgotten them. The first Christmas of his recollection he'd been given an electric train, complete with engine and caboose, along with a dozen cars, twenty-four feet of electric track, six crossing arms raised and lowered for the train, along with a whole town in the middle of it, with tiny people eating in a restaurant and nicely dressed people inside a church in which electric candles flickered. There was even a glass pond with three swans floating on it and, beyond that, a forest with miniature birds and birds' nests in the branches of the trees, as well as a few hand-painted wolves and bears and a small herd of deer.

He'd never liked the attic, especially the very back of it, where other people's things, or things he'd forgotten from the past, were kept out of sight. Many of the boxes were mislabeled. LINENS contained only one embroidered pillowcase. Under that pillowcase there was a collection of bibs and bottles. HALLOWEEN was full of plastic Easter eggs that had been opened and emptied of whatever they'd held. In a box with his mother's name on it, he'd found a little blue baby hat, a tiny pair of baby-blue socks stuffed into a pair of white leather baby shoes, with scuffed toes.

Someone had worn those. Probably himself. But since Alex would have been a baby then, of course he wouldn't remember them. But there was also a snowsuit, big enough for a kindergartner, in a box with his own name on it. The snowsuit was red. There was a pair of orange swimming trunks, which, when Alex would have been large enough to wear them, he would have been old enough to remember, he supposed. And a yo-yo—a scarlet red Duncan that had never been taken out of its package, although the paper part of the package was yellowed and curled.

He wasn't sure what he was looking for, just something he might want to ship back to Philadelphia. A photo album? He was heading back in two days, and despite his father's offer to let Alex have anything in the house he'd like, Alex had been unable to find anything, and this embarrassed him. He didn't want his father to have to consider what that meant about how unsentimental his only son felt about the mansion in which he'd been raised, full of expensive things, not one of which he wanted or could imagine taking back to his condominium with him.

8

"What did I just tell you to do?"

After Richie got out of the pool, he looked down at his own wet feet and mumbled what he knew she'd told him to do. "You told me I have to go to the potty with you and Alex or go stand by the picnic basket."

"So which is it going to be?" his mother asked.

"Picnic basket."

Richie started to trudge toward it.

"Okay," his mother said as she began to walk toward the potty with Alex. "We'll be right back. You *stay put*. Understand?"

Richie wanted to ask, again, *why*? But he didn't.

But why couldn't his mother change Alex's diaper in the grass area?

Why couldn't Richie swim in the pool without her watching? He'd passed his Tadpole class! And there was a lifeguard! His mother couldn't be seeing him anyway from her lawn chair, even if she said she could. What difference did it make if he stayed in the water for a few seconds while she and Alex were in the potty?

As he walked away from the pool, water streamed out of Richie's hair, into his eyes, off his orange swim trunks, leaving a path on the cement behind him. He'd *just gotten into the water.* He passed that girl with her red hair all flattened down and darker and practically down past her bottom. She was standing with her toes curled around the side of the pool, pointing her hands in front of her, getting ready to dive in, and this made him even more angry. She had so much more time than he had! Everything went so much faster for her! She'd been a hundred million miles behind them on her bike when he first saw her! He started to stomp. And then he heard someone call down from overhead, "Hey! Buddy! Slow down."

Richie stopped himself so fast he almost slipped. He looked up.

The lifeguard:

She was looking down at him.

Everything stopped.

The whistle she twirled got stuck in the air and stayed there. Her mouth was open, and it stayed open. Her lips were pink and shiny. She took her sunglasses off, and her eyes stuck onto his eyes. He couldn't move, and she didn't move. She was going to stare at him forever. He couldn't even blink. That little girl had already dived into the pool, right next to the painted warning NO DIVING. She put her sunglasses back on then and he could see it all in her tear-shaped mirrors—someone slipping down the slide, someone catching the beach ball, someone jumping into the air with his arms around his knees, and the huge splash of that—while he could also see himself, not moving at all. Not even blinking.

This is what it meant to be suspended, he thought.

But then she smiled and nodded. Her silver whistle flickered and started to spin again. She said, "You weren't running yet, but you were moving so fast I thought you were going to start. No running. You can keep going, just not so fast."

Just not so fast.

Richie waited until the lifeguard looked away from him before he let himself continue to the picnic basket—very, very, very slowly. He got to the gate and opened it, since he knew how, and then he walked (slowly) through the hard grass, passing the moms in their hats, toward the towel he knew was his (blue and red and white) and the picnic basket he recognized. He kept his back to the pool, staring down at the magazine his mother had left flopped open on the seat of her lounge chair. On the front of it, a lady was smiling and bringing a popsicle to her mouth, surrounded by words. On the back, a bottle of bright green shampoo had a pearl in the middle of it, sinking down and down and down into the shampoo he'd seen on TV and knew was so thick that a pearl took a hundred years to get to the bottom after you dropped it in. *Prell.*

He stood for a long time before he sat down on the towel.

Then, he sat down on the towel forever.

They were never coming back.

It would take his mother so long to change Alex's diaper that it would be Adult Swim again before he could get back into the water.

They were going to leave him sitting there with his toes in the grass until he was an old man.

He picked up one of his feet to look more closely at his toes:

They were all shriveled up!

They were *already* an old man's toes!

Then he looked at his fingertips.

They were as wrinkly as Mrs. Friedlander's face!

He was getting older and older as more and more time passed and the other children laughed and splashed in the pool without him, and even more time passed, like that pearl that was forever trying to sink through the green shampoo but never could, while his mother and Alex were somewhere too far away to come back before he was an old person who was dead. They were inside the cinderblock bathroom next to the snack bar. *Slow down,* the lifeguard had told him while he was going too fast at the side of the pool, so Richie Manning had slowed down, but now he couldn't. Now his whole life was starting to happen too fast, but his mother and Alex were moving too slow to stop his whole life from being over before he could get back in the pool before Adult Swim! Soon, he would already have been everywhere in the world—Yellowstone like next summer, Dallas like Daddy!

But then there was a shadow, and it said, "Okay, Richie. You can go swim some more now," from somewhere above and behind him.

His mother was back.

She had no idea how long she'd been gone or what had happened.

Richie stood up and held his hands out to her and said, "Look at my wrinkled hands!"

She looked at them and said, "I see, Richie. You don't have to shout."

But he was still holding them out to her to look at, and Alex, from where he was perched on their mother's hip looked at them, too.

"You were gone forever!" Richie said. "Look how old I got."

His mother laughed. She touched the top of his head. She said, "Now you can go back to the pool, my little old man."

9

Some afternoons, when Theresa took her lunch break, she'd meet her fiancé for lunch down by the pond at the center of the Ameri-Way complex. Sometimes, at the center of that pond, there paddled two large swans, behind whom paddled smaller swans.

That day Theresa had made herself a sandwich she didn't feel like eating—turkey breast (sliced so thin you could have seen through each piece of meat if you held it up to the sun) and Wonder Bread, which wasn't even like food, she thought, which was made of air, which was the kind of thing only a ghost or an angel could live on, something not constrained by the laws of gravity, something that needed no food, no body.

That turkey's white breast.

That turkey's pale death.

That bird sliced into weightlessness between two slices of weightless bread.

"Not hungry?" her fiancé asked her, his mouth full of rye bread and corned beef.

"Not really," Theresa said.

She watched the swans, who were watching her. They wanted to be fed.

Theresa stood up then and walked to the edge of the pond, but she stopped before the grass got too soggy so that the heels of her black pumps wouldn't get stuck in that muck.

She could smell the marigolds in the garden beyond the pond.

The marigolds were the smell of a mouth in the morning and rotting vegetables in a garbage can.

She tore off a piece of bread from her sandwich and tossed it to the swans. The parents parted to let one of their swan children gobble it down.

She tore off four pieces and tossed all of them in at once—a bit of bread for everyone—but, again, the parents paddled out of the way and let the babies scoop the soggy stuff up in their beaks. Then she tore up the rest of the two slices of bread and, using both hands, threw all the pieces into the pond at the same time, tossing them in such a way that they would be spread out evenly over the pond, tossing both wide and far, and still the larger swans only paddled away, stared straight ahead at Theresa, while their cygnets went from one piece of bread to the other until all of it was gone.

Only later, after kissing her fiancé goodbye and telling him she'd be meeting him at the parking lot right about five o'clock, after going back up the stairs, after sitting behind her desk, after opening her top drawer to take out the ink pad and the rubber stamp, after moving toward her a pile of forms and letters and envelopes did she see that it was gone: her ring.

No.

Theresa closed her eyes and willed herself not to cry, and in that darkness inside of her, she saw it sinking slowly to the bottom of the pond. Fish glanced in its direction as it traveled down to weedy muck into which it would settle, forever. A bit of brightness no one except Theresa would ever know was there.

10

The lifeguard twirled her silver whistle on its lanyard. It was, she thought, an aid to concentration, something mindless to do with one's hand while watching, waiting. And it felt official, like the white word LIFEGUARD printed on the front and back of her black bathing suit. It came with the role, along with the polarized sunglasses and the white stripe of zinc oxide she painted on overly sunny days across the bridge of her nose to keep that thin skin from burning and, later, peeling.

She looked at her watch. It was 12:55. In five minutes she'd have to blow the whistle for Adult Swim, hear the groaning of the children in the pool, who had to get out of the water for fifteen minutes. Then, while the housewives bobbed between the shallow and the deep end and a few of the fitter members swam their laps, she might take her break. Danny Applegate often had a milkshake waiting for her beside a soggy grilled cheese on a paper plate, so she wouldn't have to wait in the long line.

She looked at her watch again. 12:58.

In a flash of sudden bright red, a little girl came running out of the gate between the picnic area and the pool, like a horse that had just been let out of a stall. She went straight toward the shallow end, her red hair waving around behind her, and the lifeguard held her whistle to her mouth and took a breath, too late. The girls feet pushed her straight off the words NO DIVING, and she plunged with her arms out ahead of her, head first, into the shallow end.

The lifeguard held her breath and kept her eyes on the spot where the girl would most likely emerge, until she saw that she had. Her red hair was plastered to her forehead and back. She hadn't hurt herself. No broken neck. No head injury. The girl slapped her forearms across the surface of the water, headed for the deeper end.

It was too late to discipline the girl. But she blew her whistle then, a few minutes early, for Adult Swim, and stood up. If she saw the red-haired girl in time, she would be able to remind her, *No diving!* But the red-haired girl was lost now among the others, groaning, some of the most obedient and defeated making their way toward the stairs or ladders or edges of the pool in lazy laps. Others hurried up the slide's steps for one last trip down it, while those too far behind them turned away, scowling, shoulders sagging.

In under a minute, the pool was empty, as some of the mothers, tossing their sun hats on the grass, wearing their Jackie Kennedy sunglasses, and the older members, in their bathing caps and saggy swim trunks, began to move toward the water. Then they began to ease their slow, adult bodies into the blue.

Eight

10

I did not appear to be sober to Bethany.

"How fucked up are you?" she asked me after I sat down in Wolfie's chair—which had been his father's—across from her.

"I'm fine," I said. "How did you get here?"

"I drove."

"But how did you know where—"

Bethany just stared at me. Her hair wasn't in the usual ponytail. It was loose around her shoulders, which made her look even younger than she was. She wore a mini skirt with high black boots. A tight gray sweater. No bra. (I could see her nipples.) I didn't realize until I realized that I was being seen by her that I was wearing only a black slip I'd bought to wear under a too-transparent dress Wolfie had bought me for my birthday—gauzy gray, embroidered with wildflowers—which I'd never worn, since I'd been saving it for a special occasion.

My feet were bare. I kept my eyes on those. I'd painted my toenails red a week earlier. Now, most of the polish had chipped away. I could see, on the top of my left foot, a purple vein. It seemed to squirm beneath the thin skin.

"You look like shit," Bethany said. Then she laughed. "I'm sorry," she said, "but you should know this: you look like total shit."

"I'm sorry," I said.

I was. I said, "I didn't expect anyone to stop by or—"

"Care?"

I looked up from my bare feet then.

"No," I said. "I just didn't expect anyone would have to look at me."

"I don't have to look at you," Bethany said. "I just wanted to see you. I'd apologize for what I said at the meeting, but I'm not sorry."

"Okay," I said. "I didn't expect you to apologize. I'm not angry."

"What does make you angry?"

I shook my head noncommittally. I looked back down at my toes again. I shrugged.

Finally, I said, "I don't know. Why?"

"Would you be angry if I told you that last night I told the group, when you didn't show up, your real name? And what I found out about you?"

I swallowed. My throat felt as if it was swelling closed, but I said, "How did you know my real name?"

"Sorry," Bethany said. "You left your purse next to the sink in the church basement bathroom. I didn't know it was yours, so I had to look in it, go through your wallet for ID. I found your driver's license. I saw your photograph. It was an old one, apparently. You changed your hair. You never told us you were from Mission Hills, Michigan. That's where my mother grew up." She paused. She said, "Are you angry now?"

My heart was beating hard in my chest, but I managed to say, "No. I'm not angry."

"Would it surprise you to know that nobody—as in *nobody*—cared about your past?"

"I didn't expect anyone to care," I said.

"I'm not telling you no one *cares* about *you*. I'm saying that no one cares about who you were or what you did. The reason I'm here is because they asked me to find you, to tell you that."

I wanted to stand up, but I felt dizzy even as I sat back down, afraid I'd fall to my knees or faint if I rose to my feet.

"Thank you," I said. It wasn't the first time someone had tried to comfort me for what they assumed was some guilt or shame from which I suffered.

But I didn't feel grateful, and my thank you didn't sound grateful.

"Aren't you going to ask me how I found out?"

"I guess," I said. "How?"

"Like I said, my mother is from your hometown. She remembered it."

I stood up.

I was going to have to ask her to leave.

But Bethany went on. "My mother wanted me to tell you that you did the right thing. My mother got raped by her cousin and says she wished she'd stabbed him, too."

"Please," I said. "You have to go."

Bethany was nothing like I'd thought she was.

I'd thought she was tormented—the child she'd had to give up for adoption, the year of her life she'd lost in prison—but she wasn't. She was, I realized, looking at her eyes—how her pupils seemed to swell and shrink as she smirked at me—the angriest person I'd ever met in my life.

My whole body had started to shake. She stood up, seemed ready to embrace me, but I took a step backward and gestured at the door.

"Why?" Bethany asked.

"I don't feel well."

Then Bethany sounded angry:

"No one *feels well*," she said. "We all feel like crap all the time, all of us alcoholics. You don't have any excuses that everyone else doesn't have. So you've had some trouble. So what? Who hasn't? Let's get you cleaned up. You can't be seen in the state you're in now. Your hair!"

I touched my hair. I used my fingers to dig into it. It had grown, but it was still short. I felt my skull under it. I hadn't thought about my hair—brushing it or dying or washing it—since Wolfie left.

"Come on. Let's get you showered. Let's get you dressed. Let's dye your hair, for God's sake. Your roots are showing."

She pulled a box of hair dye—Clairol 250, Midnight Black—out of her bag and said, "Come on. This shit cost me five dollars, and I'm sure as hell not going to use it."

"Are you a hairdresser?" I asked her, feeling weak. Letting go. She was going to take charge now, and I was going to let her.

"I'm a stylist," she said. "And I specialize in cleaning up messes."

9

The lifeguard's mother called Father Mike. He came to the house that afternoon. By then the lifeguard had begun to wake from the drugs that had been slipped into the pulsing blue vein in the crook of her elbow, but she didn't seem to recognize him. When the priest tried to touch her hand, she pulled it away as if he'd held a match to it. After that, he came back every day for a week, but even after the drugs had worn off, she pretended not to see him or hear him.

The priest stopped his visits when she told him she hated Jesus and hated the Virgin Mary. She hated all the saints, especially the one after whom she'd been named.

Father Mike was sixty-three years old, but until then, he'd never seen such a crisis of faith or heard such expressions of anguished rage hurled at himself—himself as the representative of all the holy things that had failed them all—and he understood that sometimes there was no salvation, that sometimes there were souls it was impossible to save.

8

Becca recalled the clean sky of that afternoon, how empty it was, how the sun was shining with no obstructions whatsoever onto the aqua surface of the pool.

She remembered Chum Rogers and the stiff little flags he'd handed out to the children after the rocket launch. She'd taken one from his fat hand but left it by the fence when she got back in the water. It was gone by the time she got out—a matter of only two minutes before the lifeguard blew her whistle and shouted "Adult Swim!" But Becca didn't care about that. What would she do with the miniature flag? It was the kind of thing a boy might want, but Becca didn't care about flags.

By the time Becca got out of the pool and went through the gate toward the place she'd left her towel, her mother and Chrissy were there. Becca must have frowned, seeing them, because her mother stopped smiling and narrowed her eyes. Chrissy slapped her own face with her hands and squealed when she saw Becca. Becca looked away so she could pretend she hadn't seen how happy her stepsister was to see her, so she wouldn't have to act like she was happy, too.

They didn't even like the pool.

Why were they there?

"Why are you here?" Becca asked her mother.

"Why not? I want to get some exercise," her mother said.

She stood up from her chair then and picked up her pink bathing cap. There was no way her mother was going to be able to stuff all her hair into the cap. Why did she even bother? Pulling that rubber thing down on her head, her mother walked past her and told Becca to stay with Chrissy while she swam some laps.

"Did you eat any lunch?" she asked Becca.

"Not yet," Becca answered.

"Get yourself and Chrissy something at the snack bar. You can just charge it to the membership card."

Becca already knew this. Her stepfather had told her to do that, and she didn't need her mother there to tell her.

Did her mother tell her that she'd heard the lifeguard warn Becca not to dive off the side of the pool into the shallow end, and that if she did it again it would be the last time Becca would ever be allowed to come to the pool?

Chrissy didn't like the lifeguard, either. Every time the whistle was blown, Chrissy cringed. And she didn't like her grilled cheese sandwich. She threw it in the grass, where it took only a couple minutes for a million ants to find it.

That sandwich was made of ants before Becca's mother got out of the pool, and her mother didn't even stay in the pool until Adult Swim was over.

"You didn't get much exercise," Becca said as her mother walked toward them. She'd taken off the pink swim cap, wrestling it painfully off her head, out of her hair.

"You didn't get Chrissy any lunch," her mother said in return, and Becca pointed to the sandwich of ants in the grass.

And then the whistle blew again, and Becca didn't say anything to her mother or Chrissy. She hurried toward the chaos, all of the children heading into the water at once while the old lady and a few mothers and a man who was made of leather stepped out of the way and the lifeguard shouted, "Slow down! Slow down!"

And then the wild white froth when she jumped in, and when she kicked herself back up, and the others frothing, too, and all their arms and legs and gasps and shouts. In the pool, everyone was together but also alone. No one needed a friend in the pool, like you did on a playground. You could hold your breath and slip under the water, and no matter how many feet and elbows you saw around you, there was mostly just the sound of your own self, the other swimmers not even knowing you were there.

Her own red hair floated around her, soft and slow and strange.

And changed.

Like everything else down there.

Even the sharp edges of everything became soft.

Even the rough boys looked harmless—suspended, silenced, slowed.

Becca saw a boy's orange swim trunks slip down his hips and the bright white of his butt crack. He'd been laughing as he dog-paddled, but then he slipped under the surface. Becca, with her eyes open, could see him through the water. He was wearing an expression on his face like a crazy person's—eyes wide, cheeks puffed out.

He was looking straight at Becca with that stupid face, looking at Becca like he knew her.

7

Just after Alex Manning turned nine, he found a photo album in the attic. He hadn't gone up into the attic to look for a photo album. He'd gone up to the attic because he thought he'd left a flashlight in it.

Alex didn't like the attic, even though his friends would beg him to let them climb up there and into the cupola above it. From the road passing by, you could see that little perch, and everyone knew that the brick house behind the steel iron fence, the one with the fountains and the cupola, was the Brody Mansion, where the Mannings lived. That cupola looked like a bell tower from the road, or a spy's hideout, and any friends he invited over would ask to climb into it, to look out of it.

Alex had no idea what his mother had done with the photo album after he'd hurried out of the attic with it, into her bedroom, holding it out, pointing at a boy he somehow knew, but from another place and time, with dark curls, wearing a striped shirt, sitting with the baby he recognized as himself in his lap on the couch in some living room he also knew he'd been in—something about the color of the walls, the light pouring in through a window.

Alex was, in the snapshot of himself as the infant he'd once been, looking into the face of an older boy in whose lap he sat. In the mirror hanging over the couch behind the two of them there was a starburst turning into the burned-out blue of a flash cube, and inside that starburst was his mother's face. Alex could see her dark hair and her smile and the kind of orange dress without sleeves he know that, once, she used to wear, and he held it out in front of him and said, "Mom! I found him! That boy! Remember? This is him!"

She pulled the album out of Alex's hands and slammed it shut on the snapshot of that boy and Alex, both of them smiling in front of the explosion of their mother's smile in front of them, reflected in the mirror behind them.

6

Richard wanted to show Richie how it all worked, so he drew a diagram.

He drew, first, the rocket (Saturn V) and its three parts. He explained how the first part alone consisted of five engines—each of which produced seven million pounds of thrust, and how this thrust would propel the astronauts off Earth fast enough to escape this planet's gravity. Then, the first of the three parts would detach.

"What happens to it then?" Marie asked.

"I don't know, Marie. It burns up, I guess."

He was about to describe the second part of the rocket, but Marie asked what would happen if the first did *not* burn up or fall into the ocean, but instead crashed back to Earth. Couldn't a whole city be destroyed by something like that? Or someone's neighborhood? Someone's house?

Richard loved his wife, but he wished she'd gone to college. But even in high school she hadn't excelled. She couldn't be blamed. Her parents were uneducated. And she'd been busy taking care of her siblings and cleaning the house after her father left and her mother had to go to work cleaning other people's houses.

But thanks to him, Marie had leisure time now. There were the boys, of course, but that wasn't a full-time job, like his.

If she had any interest, she could certainly have read something other than cookbooks and women's magazines and Dr. Spock's *Baby & Child Care.*

Richard was, he realized, married to a woman who was more afraid that their house would be blown up by a discarded part of the lunar module than she was interested in the fact that in a few days the first steps by any human being were about to be taken on the moon.

This didn't surprise him, but it annoyed him, given the enormous scope of what was about to happen—historically, nationally, even *personally.* It made him wish his father was alive to witness this. The old man had always had such faith in his country, the future in which his son and grandsons—

Who even knew what Richie might be able do or be or achieve?

What was one city, one neighborhood, one house lost in the context of such monumental achievement? What was some speck of destruction on Earth caused by rocket debris falling on someone's garage in comparison to what this mission meant for humanity—and, most importantly (why didn't she think of this?), for their sons?

"It just seems like something could go wrong, not just for the astronauts, but for someone else."

Richard slapped his pencil down on his drawing and said, "Gee, I think they've probably thought that out at NASA, Marie. But if you're concerned, you should give Cape Kennedy a call."

Marie flushed.

She got up from the table, pretending there was some reason she needed to fill the kettle with water.

Since when did they start drinking tea after dinner?

Richie asked where the astronauts would sleep, and why had they changed the name of the Lunar Module to *Eagle* from *Snoopy*. Richie had liked the first name better.

"Well, son. Think about that. Doesn't the *Eagle* sound more serious and important than the *Snoopy*?"

Richie didn't answer. Either he didn't want to tell Richard what he thought about the *Eagle* compared to the *Snoopy*, or he was taking his time, considering this.

"Well, anyway," Richard said. "That's what the scientists at NASA thought, and I trust them. These are men who've dedicated their whole lives to this mission."

This last part was for Marie's benefit, not Richie's, and she knew it.

Richard looked at his wife.

The dark hair. The heart-shaped face with two red stripes of what he hoped was anger on her cheeks but which he worried might be shame.

"I'm sorry, Marie," Richard said. "I didn't mean to snap at—"

"Please!" she said. "I don't care!"

No, she didn't care.

Well, probably, a wife's interests should be bound to Earth. The children. The lawn. The roof. The ants in the kitchen. The secretaries at his office had loudly proclaimed that there was no way they would marry, or stay married to, a man on his way to the moon: "Can you even *imagine*?!"

Richard had pointed out that there were plenty of women married to Marines who were getting shot in Vietnam, and he asked if no man with a dangerous job should have a wife.

They scoffed. They said *that* was different. *Those* men at least had a *chance* of coming back. You could fight an enemy, but good luck fighting space! And it had only been two years since they'd pulled the charred remains of those other astronauts out of Apollo 1. Didn't anyone remember *that*? And at least those men had been on Earth when they died. Who was going to pull the charred remains of astronauts out of a capsule when it burned up on the moon?

But, clearly, those secretaries were all in love with the astronauts. Every woman in the US (maybe in the whole world) was in love with them, especially with Armstrong and Aldrin. Collins was the least romantic, since he'd be the one orbiting while the other two walked on the moon.

Maybe it was good to have a wife like Marie. The girl he'd dated before he met Marie had left him for a prizefighter—the only prizefighter anyone at their college had ever met.

She had been a risk-taker.

Richard imagined that ex-girlfriend now, lying in bed beside her prizefighter, reading every word she could find about Buzz and Neil. He should be grateful to be married to a woman who wouldn't leave him for a prizefighter or a racecar driver or an astronaut.

Still, Richard needed Richie to be excited, to *want* to go to the moon one day—since, one day, he might very well have the opportunity to do exactly that!

5

The lifeguard didn't seem to notice Richie Manning as she passed him on her way to the snack bar, taking her break for Adult Swim. But he noticed himself reflected in her big sunglasses, shaped like tear drops. He recognized his own face, although it was spread out and doubled, and he didn't look like himself. He looked like someone who looked like himself.

But that had happened to him before, and not just in the funny mirrors that made you fat and then skinny when you stood in front of them at the fair. You could move around inside those mirrors and make your face collapse into a thin line, crouch a little and your face would spread out like cookie dough when it got rolled with a wooden pin on waxed paper. You could make your forehead ten times wider than the whole rest of your body. But you still knew it was you, since you knew things about yourself that you didn't need to recognize to know they were yours—the way he could find his own face in photographs of himself as a baby. Or the way that during the Christmas performance, he stood on the stage and looked out at all the moms in the audience and the only face with light on it was his mother's.

Some little girl whined at the lifeguard, "How long?"

"Not long!" the lifeguard said but kept walking so that they all knew that even if she turned around right that minute, climbed back into her chair and blew the whistle, it would take her longer than *Not Long.*

And she was headed in the opposite direction of Not Long.

She was headed in the direction of *Not Yet,* leaving Richie and the girl who'd whined and all the other children (more children than had ever been at the Jolly Rogers Swim Club all together on the same afternoon) to wait, their faces and bellies pressed against the chain-link fence.

Mrs. Friedlander patted him on the head as she passed him on her way to that gate. Then, she was gone. She was in the pool. He could see her rubber flowers traveling a straight path through the water from one side of it to the other, following exactly the thick black line painted on the bottom.

And Richie realized then, even if no one else did, that the rope between the deep end and the shallow end wasn't there because usually he liked the part where the grown-ups swimming had to dive under it while they swam, and how it sometimes took old people like Mrs. Friedlander a couple seconds after that to come back to the surface to restart their very slow, very regular rhythm of arms and kicks and breaths.

Maybe the rope was broken.

It didn't matter.

A rope would not have saved Richie Manning, who knew exactly where the shallow end turned into the deep end.

It got darker there.

You didn't need a rope to see where that darkness started.

Also, the closer you got to it, the colder the water got. And he wouldn't go there because he didn't want to be in the colder and darker part yet and because he knew he'd get in trouble, since the lifeguard would see he was too little to have passed the Goldfish class, and even if some kids even littler *had* passed it and were allowed to swim on the other side of the rope, she'd be able to see that Richie wasn't swimming the way you were supposed to after you passed your Goldfish class—the way Mrs. Friedlander swam, with straight arms and her body spread out flat. He was learning. He could reach and pull. But he couldn't breathe. The lifeguard would know he was only a Tadpole because of how he couldn't breathe.

For a few minutes it was just a few of them—Mrs. Friedlander, the leather man, and his old neighbor—who were actually swimming. A mother with a baby inside her stomach sat beside another woman, both wearing their straw hats, dangling their legs just up to the knees in the water as they sat at the side of the pool. They were talking and talking and talking.

But then he saw another lady.

She was starting out at the deep end, getting ready, maybe, to dive in instead of wading into the shallow end like Mrs. Friedlander did.

This lady had a pink swimming cap, and she was wearing a black bathing suit with a ruffly skirt around her rear end and the tops of her legs. She stood there forever, wrestling that pink cap onto her head. She made a face like *ouch* as she tried to stuff her too-much-too-long-black-hair into it.

You could tell it hurt, and also that she'd never get it all up there.

She stopped trying, and then she just stood and stared at the water for a million years, maybe finishing some long thought in her head, maybe thinking that she had time, that Adult Swim would last forever, which made Richie want to make that pulled-hair noise, because even this grown-up knew that Adult Swim would never end.

He saw how she took a deep breath, and then he did, too, and he held it in his lungs the way she did, and when she bent over and slipped into the blue and started to skim across it, Richie felt like he *was* her.

Richie felt himself inside her body, feeling what her body was feeling, how cold and floaty it was, how sweet it tasted, and the sting of that sweetness in her nose, and then she was moving smoothly, and even though Richie had never learned to swim like that, he knew exactly how that felt—that you were your other self, your *real* self, the self that was always inside of you and only got out when you were in the pool. Now you were the *you* that got poured out, like Tang poured out of the plastic jug and into the thermos, out of the thermos into its little cup.

The light was you, and the sounds you made became a silence that was also a sound:

Whoosh.

4

Mrs. Nixon was asked to pick from his closet the most funereal of her husband's suits for him, and to accompany him down to the Oval Office after he was dressed and his hair was combed. She preferred to powder her husband's forehead, nose, and upper lip herself, having one too many times found the President to appear embalmed, far too chalky, after that day's makeup woman had passed a puff over him—too much powder, laid on too thick, too broadly. Mrs. Nixon would do it herself, and if they tried to redo it after the cameras were set up, she would protest.

"Yes! Give us half an hour," Pat said.

She took her husband's hand.

The mood was more than festive.

All of them, particularly the interns and the staff who so rarely had the chance to gather with the First Family around a television set, had become childlike in their elation, whispering to one another and then laughing hysterically, guiltily, and hugging each other. They'd just watched, *in color*, the three astronauts as they tumbled around, seeming to be swimming in circles through very clear water, while wearing the white uniforms of bakers, wielding the tools of car mechanics in their bare hands. One astronaut was indistinguishable from the next, just a leg, a hand, the side of a face as they opened the lunar module in silence and slow motion. Just a dull hum accompanied their operations. It was hard to know what was happening. A flashlight was pointed at a wheel.

When there was finally a clear voice saying first, something that couldn't be understood, followed by, ". . . almost got the probe out . . ." and then, "Yeah, it looks good . . . there's some bright spots shining on the probe . . . just enough for us to make it out."

More hum, and then, "Okay, comin' down."

"Roger."

"Beautiful picture we got now, Houston."

Gradually, on the television, a white spot grew closer and closer until it filled the screen, fuzzily. At first it appeared to be the beam of a miniature flashlight, and then they realized it must be the moon, and then it began to lose its round shape and clear outlines.

An astronaut's elbow?

"TV cable's getting in the way."

"We see lotsa arms."

Two white boots.

And the dot returned. Glowing.

And then a hatch.

A tunnel?

"The lighting looks good to us, Houston."

They were swimming toward a darkness, blurrily.

"That sounds fine to us, over."

Then, silence that might have sounded like space, which might have sounded like death, began, after which those gathered around the White House television set said nothing more, became their own silence. There was not even the sound that might be made by the nylon-against-nylon of a woman's thighs rubbing against each other when she shifted her weight from one foot to other, until a smoker coughed dryly into his fist, and Judy Agnew, who stood beside her husband, who stood beside the wife of the President—all three of them transfixed by the television screen—turned and gave the man (she'd forgotten his name—some kind of organizer, a writer, who could possibly keep these people straight?) a very cold look.

The astronauts swam on, noted something "burned out" that "should be okay tomorrow," and then a few more Overs, Rogers, and the screen went black, and the President turned the knob on the television, it went blank, and he turned around and shouted, "Here we come, Moon! We're gonna get you!" and then laughter, chatter, unabashed laughter and sobs, and everyone cheered as they watched the President put his arm at the waist of the First Lady and kiss her firmly on the lips.

Then he was handed his "just in case" speech. The cameramen were waiting.

"Better safe than sorry," the President said. Then he tried to stop smiling and to imagine that something that would never happen already had as he took the speech with him and headed for the Oval Office.

3

It wasn't just while on the telephone with Richard that morning, Marie knew. Richie truly hadn't seemed excited by the liftoff, the astronauts, or the dream of Americans walking on the moon.

Both of her sons would've taken more interest in the show the Puppet Lady put on at the public library every Wednesday morning, which Richie had expressed shock and disappointment about having to miss. Marie had assured him that the puppet show would not be taking place, given that this was the morning that a rocket ship full of astronauts was taking off for the *moon,* and even the Puppet Lady would be home watching that on television.

And, of course, he'd have far preferred to get to the pool earlier than seeing either the Puppet Lady or the rocket launch. Richie would even have preferred a comic book about rockets than to be told to sit still on the floor in the living room in front of the television, waiting for the liftoff, which required far more time than anything suspenseful could take and remain suspenseful.

How much preparation it had taken!

Even after they'd been assured by Walter Concrete that *everything is prepared, everything is in place,* it took forever for the rocket to launch.

How much talk prefaced the fireball and the scaffolding falling away! And, even then, how very, very slowly that rocket seemed to rise into the air—rising, rising, rising, until it simply disappeared.

"Is it done yet?" Richie asked after the rocket slipped away from their television screen.

"Yes!" Marie had said. "Wasn't that exciting?"

Richie didn't answer her.

She was glad that Richard wasn't there after all.

2

Richie hadn't wanted to go to kindergarten. Then, he'd loved kindergarten—except that all winter his mother made him wear gloves to school every morning, and he couldn't move his fingers around inside of them. When he told her that he wanted to wear mittens instead of gloves, she said that mittens wouldn't keep his fingers warm enough. She'd known a little boy like Richie once, long ago, whose mittens got wet, and his fingers got frostbitten.

Frostbit.

Like if a dog bit you, or a wolf, but like the bite was made of cold instead of teeth.

So, some afternoons when Richie got home, even though it had only taken him a few minutes to get there, he might be in a bad mood. He might yank off the gloves and throw them on the floor and say, "I can't move my fingers!"

Finally, his father said to his mother, "For God's sake, let the boy wear mittens!"

West Mission Elementary School had a hill. The hill started outside the dark kindergarten window that seemed, on a Saturday, not to be the same room in which he spent his other afternoons, even if it was. The hill ended at a wooden fence between someone's backyard and the playground. Richie was trying to tell his mother that he couldn't pull his sled with its rope with his hands in the gloves because the gloves' fingers made his own fingers too fat to move.

Then, after his father told Marie that Richie should be allowed to wear mittens, Richie was allowed to wear mittens.

Then, he went sledding.

His sled was plastic, red, and very fast. His aunt had given it to him for Christmas. If a friend was in it with him, the sled was heavier, so it was even faster, and it went even faster when the snow was packed down after a hundred other sleds had already gone down it. Sometimes you might crash into the wooden fence and fall off your sled with your face in the snow, laughing. But once, Anne Snyder got her nose broken doing that, and even though everyone heard her screams, they ignored her because the red splash of her blood in the snow was the same color as her scarf, so they thought she was screaming because her scarf fell off.

1

Even with all the water pouring off his dark curls and down his face and back and chest, the lifeguard could see tears spring into the little boy's eyes.

She was the lifeguard, after all, and he was a Tadpole, and she'd caught him breaking a rule. No Running. But the boy hadn't known he was running until the lifeguard called down to him, “Hey, buddy! No running! Okay?”

She was glad she hadn’t had to blow the whistle to get his attention, since not only did the whistle get the attention of the kid who was breaking the rules, it got the attention of everyone else at the pool, and then their attention became fixed on the one who’d broken the rule. This didn’t bother her with the older ones, who were standing on railings or dunking each other too roughly or who’d somehow smuggled a hard ball—football, basketball—into the pool and were throwing it around all those smaller children, who were swimmingly oblivious, and for whom the rule existed, so that they didn’t pop out of the water saying, “Marco!” to be slammed in the side of the head by a football thrown by a thirteen-year-old with nearly actual grown-man muscles.

But she hated to embarrass the little girls, holding their arms in a triangle out in front of them, getting ready to attempt the first head-first dives of their lives, as they stood (some of them not yet able to read, she supposed) on the stenciled warning: SHALLOW END, NO DIVING. The shriek of the whistle, and how startled they seemed, how horrified at themselves. And, to make it worse, usually the child’s mother came marching through the gate, maybe still holding a damp copy of *Good Housekeeping* in her hand, its pages wrinkling and flapping at her thighs, and grabbed the little girl by the arm and pulled her out, saying things to her no one needed to hear to understand: *You’re in big trouble, young lady. You’re having a time out. You know the rules. What’s wrong with you?*

But, in truth, it was rarely a girl who had a whistle blown at her.

Luckily, she’d been able to catch this boy’s attention before anyone but him needed to know of his transgression. And still, the way he stopped everything—even seemed to stop breathing—turning his face toward her, full of terror and awe and the sense of total exposure combined with disorientation, regret, self-defensiveness, mortification (which were, the lifeguard thought to herself—either in that moment or later, many times, in the years to come—the exact ingredients, each in an equal portion, that comprised the state of disgrace) and stood like a statue then, staring up at her.

She saw the pink scrape on his belly, the one he'd just gotten while pulling himself out of the pool against its cement side. It was a mild abrasion that the forensic pathologist would, that evening, touch gently with his latex glove while Richie lay naked on a steel table in the hospital basement.

At that time, the scrape on the body's torso was mostly a matter of curiosity to the pathologist. He had a diagram with the outline of a child's body on it, and he needed to draw an arrow to that spot and write something on it, note the minor injury, and theorize its cause, which was one of the most challenging, and therefore most fulfilling, of his tasks.

"Abrasion," he wrote, and drew an arrow to the outline's torso, "result of sustained attempt at resuscitation," which seemed about as good a guess as any.

It would not be for many years, after the pathologist had a child of his own, about this child's age, that he'd see exactly such an abrasion on his own boy's belly after he'd pushed himself up and out of the cement side of a swimming pool.

Then, despite all the bodies he'd examined over the years, Richie Manning's would return to him, along with the sweet smell of the inhaled chlorine that the pathologist had emptied into a basin from the boy—using, afterward, a stainless steel cup to measure the amount of water in the lungs, and would even recall, as if it were in his hand at that moment, how heavy that cup had felt when he'd placed it on the scale. How pink the young lungs were when they were first exposed. And those dark curls against the gray table.

The lifeguard smiled and shook her head, and the boy glanced away from her, at his feet, and shrugged back off to the grassy section where his mother was probably waiting for him. He had likely been summoned out of the pool to eat a sandwich, or because they needed to go home or to the grocery store, and he wasn't ready to leave.

They were never ready to leave.

Nine

1

The bright white of his butt crack, the expression on his face like a crazy person—eyes wide, cheeks puffed out, looking straight at Becca with that crazy face, as if he recognized her.

Well, Becca didn't recognize him.

She somersaulted again until she was headed away from the deep end and away from him.

He's just starting to drown, he thinks.

A rope, he thinks.

The rope.

How has he drifted past it into the deep end?

He opens his eyes wide underwater to look for it.

Then he sees—

It's red.

It flows away from a girl as she swims away from him.

Silk, streaming loose.

Just out of reach.

And then it might have been that very moment.

Yes.

She felt it then, exactly.

And then, again—

There.

There it is. And all he has to do now is paddle toward it like a dog, holding the air he'll need in his cheeks until he's pulled himself out of the water by this red rope, after his fingers have gotten ahold of it, reaching toward it with his arm, stretching his arm as far as it will go, spreading his fingers, feeling it—loose, and drifting, his fingers slipping through it even as he tries to hold it in his hand and—

Then the boy drifted down, down, moving toward the darker, colder part of the pool, where Becca knew he shouldn't be swimming, or sinking, and she could tell that he knew it, too, with his eyes wide open, puffed-up cheeks, hands paddling.

No.

He just looked curious now, but harmless. Peaceful, floating toward her with his arms outstretched, but as if he no longer needed anything from her, was content just to float in her direction, gazing at her through the blue as the water tried to tug him away, to separate them forever—thicker and more dense than you'd ever thought water would be when you were above it, diving into it, or standing with a glass of it at the sink, filling it, drinking it—but also uniting them forever.

Then she felt his fist in her hair.

Dragging her down with him.

Then she was watching him spiral slowly to the bottom of the pool.

Then she heard someone calling her name:

"Becca!"

2

Peter Campion drove past West Mission Hills High School, in which he was not teaching English that morning, having called in sick, watching the street signs. He knew she lived on Crystal Lake Drive, although her house was nowhere near Crystal Lake.

He'd only found out from the newspapers that the lifeguard's father had been a mailman, and that he'd died just a year before Richie Manning drowned. Based on that fact—the father, a mailman—he felt sure that none of the three-story houses with fountains in which naiads danced naked at the center of rolling lawns would be hers.

Although he'd taught at West Mission Hills High since he'd finished his college degree, he'd always lived outside of the "West" part of Mission Hills—in the cheaper and more dangerous neighborhoods where all the old Victorians had been chopped into one-room apartments and efficiencies, like his.

He drove past dozens of ostentatious mansions—servants' bungalows tucked in backyards, swimming pools, cast-iron fences, cupolas—and then another dozen less spectacular houses, but fabulously tasteful, and he felt, again, the difference between himself and his students.

Did they know they were rich?

Did they know that he wasn't?

Or did they assume that everyone was as rich as they were, except for maybe the Blacks and Appalachians.

That had been the impression he'd gotten from the casual way they talked about their ski villas in Aspen. If any of their fathers, except for the lifeguard's, worked anywhere other than AmeriWay, he hadn't heard about it.

His was a job he was going to have to quit, Peter Campion knew, before he got fired from it. Since September, he'd found himself moving from "losing his patience" straight to swift fury when his students were whispering or staring into space.

Then there was the incident with a paper cutter in his classroom. On a Thursday afternoon, his least favorite student, Brad Corral, managed to bring its blade down on his hand while trying to impress his friends. Peter Campion had watched that wide wrestler fall to his knees before slumping forward. He'd heard the kid's head knock hard against the cabinets (full of paper, waiting to be cut).

There'd been some snickers from the front row, and he would never know if they'd snickered after noticing what had happened or after hearing Mr. Campion say, under his breath, "Oh, fuck." But it wasn't until Peter had seen the two severed half-digits set out beside one another, as if they'd been positioned for display on the institutional green of the paper cutter's checkered surface, that he himself felt a small sneeze of laughter begin in the back of his throat. He might have been smiling as he turned to the class and shouted, "Call the office. Tell them to call an ambulance."

And then all the energy—like the Fourth of July, except that his students weren't *viewing* fireworks, they had *become* fireworks, shot into the sky, whistling and screaming and exploding into a million sparkling thumbtacks and razor blades and spiky burning snowflakes. Girls pretended to cry. Boys pretended not to guffaw.

Miss Beck had hurried to the classroom with some ice in a container. She'd picked up Brad's fingers as if they were alive, and dangerous, and placed them in the container. The nurse followed, tearing a run in her nylons while crawling across the floor with her tourniquets to reach Brad Corral. Peter had done what was expected of him—holding the boy up, shouting into his ear, "Talk to me, Brad! Tell me what year it is!"

But, again, he wanted to laugh, unforgivably, when the wrestler repeated, "What year it is."

The ambulance arrived only about four seconds before the wrestler's mother, who was wearing a fur coat—a thing made out of hundreds of little skinned animals—which also threatened to make him (most unacceptably) begin to laugh. And then Brad Corral was taken away on a stretcher and class was dismissed. The substitute janitor mopped the blood (surprisingly little) up, while shaking his head, muttering some sentence several times that contained the word *stupid*.

After that, the paper cutters were rounded up, thrown away or hidden so that there was only one that Peter himself personally knew the location of now, kept on a counter in the supply room next to the principal's office and beside the ditto machine, accessible only to those teachers who had the room's key. There, on several occasions, alone with the thing (which, he felt sure, was the very one that had sliced off his student's fingers, since he thought he could see what looked like a few black flecks of blood still stuck in the crack between the blade of it and the hinge), he found himself feeling as if he were in love with it—the indifferent swish of its arm, its ruthless efficiency.

After winding from boulevard to boulevard past the kinds of houses he imagined students like Brad Corral inhabited with their animal-draped mothers and their cigar-smoking fathers, he saw it: Crystal Lake Drive. He turned left and followed the numbers, glancing around for 1100 as the houses grew smaller and smaller, and then he saw hers—a tidy bungalow with green shutters and a brick chimney. He pulled up beside the curb and waited. He looked around. There was a flowering tree in the front yard (magnolia? dogwood?) from which the petals had fallen a few weeks earlier, it seemed, so that those petals lay now, equally distributed, in a shriveled skirt around the flowerless tree.

Then he thought he saw a shadow pass over the curtains in the front window.

Then, the front door opened, and the lifeguard stepped out wearing a dress that was both the color and the shape of a grocery bag and little white canvas shoes. She pulled the front door closed behind her and descended the two front steps.

3

She'd taken it from him and wrapped her arms around it and said, "That wasn't supposed to be in the attic. You stay out of the attic until I find out what else your aunt didn't manage to get rid of."

But Alex didn't stay out of the attic, of course. The next time he went up there, his mother was asleep, and his father was out of town. His babysitter Becca Brummler had to practice with the choir so she couldn't babysit, so he was alone.

He looked on every shelf, in every box, finding old certificates and pictures of his parents looking like thin, young strangers. They looked far too happy, holding hands, to be his parents. He found his father's high school yearbook. His father as a gray blur in the back row of the golf team photo. His father making faces in the cafeteria. He found a photo of himself on the back of one of the ponies that had been brought to their backyard in a trailer for his sixth birthday.

The photo album was gone.

But he didn't need to find it.

That image was permanently in his brain.

Alex in the lap of the boy who'd been his brother.

Alex knew all about it now without ever having been told a thing. Even before he found the album, he'd understood. Hadn't he? He had seen how, in kindergarten, Mrs. Talifero's whole body froze one day when she called him by another boy's name. Why? He'd wanted to laugh and to tell her it was fine. She was old. She was always calling her afternoon kindergartners by her morning kindergartners' names. She was always calling her students by their older brothers' or sisters' names. Why was it any different to call Alex by the wrong name?

Sometimes he had a dream that he was lost in a forest. A boy he recognized, without knowing from where, would creep out of the shadows and stretch out his arm, seeming to want to take Alex's hand. But Alex was too afraid. He would force himself to wake up then, gasping for breath. He had long since stopped trying to go in search of his mother after a nightmare. She kept the door to her bedroom locked at night. His father, when he wasn't traveling, would be sleeping too heavily to wake up if Alex slipped into bed with him, but he would also be sleeping too heavily to be any comfort.

Often it was his babysitter who woke him up from a nightmare. When his father was gone, Becca Brummler sometimes stayed overnight, sleeping in Alex's room on the special mattress his parents had put on the floor. He wanted her to sleep with him in his bed, or for her to sleep in his bed and for him to sleep below her on the floor, but these ideas just made Becca laugh.

She wore long white cotton nightgowns, and her face smelled like butter and bread as she shook him awake and told him, "Wake up, Alex. You're having a nightmare. Everything's fine. You were asleep. I'm here."

She'd almost graduated from high school, though, and was getting ready for the thing he didn't understand then—college—before he ever answered her question, "What was your nightmare?" He'd always just shrugged and said, "I don't know," because, in truth, he didn't know, until one day he said to her, "I have a brother, and he wants me to be like him. He wants me to be dead."

The look on his babysitter's face was like the expression he would see on his mother's in another year when he brought the photo album to her—but more confused, not angry, just surprised and full of wonder. She knew something he didn't know, like something hidden in a hole that had been dug out of the ground by a dog.

4

Bob Mulnix kissed his new wife goodbye that morning before she got out of bed, and she made a gentle, affectionate sound, kissing him back, falling back into a dream, lost in all her long black hair.

It was only six o'clock in the morning, and he'd known from the beginning that Lynnette liked to sleep in. She'd worked in that bar for years, starting her shift at 5:00 p.m., getting home at one in the morning, catching four or five hours of sleep—if she had a few drinks and a couple cigarettes, enough to calm her down from the chaos generated through the night, smiling at men, ignoring their crude comments, fetching their drinks, dodging their hands or, if she thought it might make the difference between a big tip or no tip, she might let the hand linger, like his own hand.

Becca was awake already when Bob passed through the kitchen.

"Becca! Up so early! Excited for the rocket launch?"

"Not really," she said.

The whites of her big blue eyes looked pink. Had she been crying?

"Is something wrong, honey?"

"No."

Becca was wearing a flannel nightgown—too hot for the weather. He'd asked Lynette to take some money out of his wallet to buy the girl a summer nightie, but apparently she never had.

"Your mom's still asleep. Do you need me to help you get some breakfast?"

"I'm not hungry yet," she said.

Why was she standing in the kitchen?

Bob didn't ask a second time. He said, "Something's wrong." Becca didn't say anything. "Where's your brother?" he asked. Because whatever was wrong seemed to him unlikely not to have to do with Davey.

Bob, unlike his wife, decided not to argue with the girl. She just needed time. He said, "Okay. I know. But what's the matter?"

"I thought you weren't going to work today. You said you'd watch the rocket with us."

"Oh, I know," Bob said, "but—"

Then he thought of all the promises that had been made to this little girl, only to be broken. He heard the toilet flush upstairs.

Davey. Lynette would be asleep several more hours. Bob said, "You're right. That's what I said. And that's what's going to happen. I'll drive in and put a sign on the door. Closed!" He snapped his fingers and laughed, but she only nodded. "I'll be home in a flash! And we'll watch that rocket launch together!"

5

To: H. R. Haldeman
From: Bill Safire
IN EVENT OF MOON DISASTER
PRIOR TO THE PRESIDENT'S STATEMENT:
NASA ENDS COMMUNICATION WITH MEN.
The President should telephone each of the widows-to-be.

STATEMENT:
Fate has ordained that the men who went to the moon to explore in peace will stay on the moon to rest in peace.

These brave men, Neil Armstrong and Edwin Aldrin, know that there is no hope for their recovery. But they also know that there is hope for mankind in their sacrifice.

These two men are laying down their lives in mankind's most noble goal: the search for truth and understanding.

They will be mourned by their families and friends; they will be mourned by their nation; they will be mourned by the people of the world; they will be mourned by a Mother Earth that dared send two of her sons into the unknown.

In their exploration, they stirred the people of the world to feel as one; in their sacrifice, they bind more tightly the brotherhood of man.

In ancient days, men looked at stars and saw their heroes in the

> constellations. In modern times, we do much the same, but our heroes are epic men of flesh and blood.
>
> Others will follow, and surely find their way home. Man's search will not be denied. But these men were the first, and they will remain the foremost in our hearts.
>
> For every human being who looks up at the moon in the nights to come will know that there is some corner of another world that is forever mankind.

6

The girl's name was not supposed to be released to the public. She was a minor. But her name was in the paper anyway because her sister, Amy (*sic*) Brummler, who'd been visiting her mother and sister from Illinois at the time of the incident, spoke to a reporter and was quoted as saying, "Becca is a very good girl. She was violated."

The stepbrother's name was in the paper, though.

David Daniels Mulnix, aged 18, died at home at 4:05 a.m. on July 27, 1969.

Becca Brummler.

It was still a small enough town that the name didn't have to be published in the paper for everyone to know whose name it would be.

7

Her parents had bought a house at the edge of the Mission Hills School District, where the small houses and duplexes were. Her mother had wanted her to go to the best possible schools, and the reason West Mission Hills had the best schools was because it was populated by some of the richest families in the state. The parents of the lifeguard's classmates drove not only Mercedes but flew their own helicopters, which they kept on landing pads that also served as the roofs of their mansions. They owned second houses in Telluride and Aspen, Colorado. None of their fathers were mailmen, and none of their fathers died.

The lifeguard was pretty, yes. And some boys liked her. But she was not a member of what the paper called the "West Missioners"—the name given to the kind of girl the paper wanted her to be: spoiled, rich, negligent.

There were those who objected. "I saw that little girl get baptized. I've gone to church with her since her parents moved to town. She is not the girl you describe."

In fact, even when the priest used his finger, dipped in cold water, to draw a cross on the infant lifeguard's forehead (*In the name of the Father, Son, and Holy Ghost*), the baby never cried. Her mother held her and shed some tears. Her father cleared his throat and folded his hands and closed his eyes. (They'd been married for many years. How long must they have prayed for a baby? And now they were too old to have another.)

And the lifeguard herself had narrowly survived a difficult delivery. She'd come into the world blue, without a heartbeat—umbilical cord wrapped around her neck. "It was a miracle," the doctor said when he told the lifeguard's father in the waiting room that it had been close, but he had a healthy daughter.

After she fled through the doors of West Mission Hills High—even as she heard Mr. Campion and the secretary, Miss Beck, calling after her—she ran home.

Four miles.

Her mother wasn't home.

The lifeguard went to the cupboard where her father had kept his shot glass and his bottle of Jim Beam, from which he'd poured himself a shot every afternoon as soon as he walked in the door after delivering mail (walking twenty miles through rain or snow or sleet), still in his blue uniform. The lifeguard would hug him, and whatever season it was—autumn, winter, spring, summer—she would smell it on him. The tinny smell of April rain. The humidity of June's magnolias. The rotting leaves of October. The emptiness of a February snowstorm. May's roses in bloom. The chlorinated scent of his sweat in July.

She hadn't opened that cupboard since his death, and wasn't sure what she'd find, but she found what had always been there, since her mother had never moved his shot glass or his nearly full bottle, untouched. Just as his slippers were still waiting for him, side by side, at the foot of her parents' bed. As far as she knew, her mother had only given away his uniforms, to his post office friends—since a postman's uniform had to be purchased with his own money, and they weren't cheap—but there was still a drawer full of thick blue socks.

She took down the bottle, which wasn't dusty but had grown a sticky resin around its neck. And the shot glass was just as she remembered it—glass, with an image of two dice seeming to have just been rolled printed on it—although she'd never held it in her own hand, and it was heavier than she expected.

She made her way to her bed and, after stumbling once or twice, hit her knee on the bedframe so that there was a bit of bleeding. She touched the blood, and it stuck to her fingertips. So she tasted it—rust and honey and orange peels.

Was that what was inside her?

And then she fell asleep on her side and didn't wake up until five o'clock that evening, when her mother came into her room and said, "There's a teacher from the school on the phone who wants to talk to you. Mr. Campion. He says he's your English teacher."

8

"Becca! *Becca!*"

How could she hear her name being called out from the center of that sound, getting louder and louder, over all the names being called, and so many mothers calling. She lifted her face out of the water and tried to see, but there were so many mothers and women and a few old men, and the snack bar boy taking off his white apron, leaving it behind him on the ground, and the lifeguard tossing her sunglasses off of her face, hurrying so quickly down from her chair that she slipped on the last rung of the ladder, and Becca saw a flash of pain cross her face, and Becca even felt it—the twisted ankle—even as the lifeguard never felt it.

And then she saw her mother was there, with her hands cupped around her mouth, wearing her black swimsuit with its floppy skirt, and Chrissy beside her mother, hanging onto a strap of her mother's suit and hardly smiling at all, until Becca was at the side of the pool, and her mother had grabbed her arm and was pulling her (too hard!) up and out of it, dragging her up and out like a bag full of soggy blankets, until Becca was lying on her stomach on the cement at her mother's feet, and Chrissy, smiling again, looked down, her eyes still full of wonder.

"Get on your feet," her mother shouted to Becca. "We're leaving right now!"

And then they were moving through the gate, not even going back to the place on the grass where Becca had left her towel or stopping into the locker room. (Her mother's purse? She was leaving that, too?)

They moved backward through time and the tunnel then, passing the girl who'd stamped Becca's hand, the one with the long black braid, who was standing up, but not moving at all, her hand covering her mouth.

Her mother opened the back of her car then and said, "Get into the back seat, get Chrissy in there, keep your head down and don't talk to anyone. I have to get my keys. But I'll be right back. I promise, Becca. Just do as I say."

It confused Becca, this strange patience of her mother's suddenly. This voice she'd only heard her mother use once before, when she'd picked up the neighbor's cat from the place in the street where a car had knocked it down, and she took the cat to the car and, like Becca, told the cat she would hurry, she promised, just lie still and don't say anything, and I'll be right back, I just have to get my keys, I promise I'll be right back, and then she and Becca and the cat bleeding in the car's back seat were rushing toward a veterinarian, and whatever happened after that was never explained to Becca, except that her mother said, "Everything is fine. We did the best we could, at least. We can always remember that: we did everything we could for the cat."

Becca pulled Chrissy in beside her and whispered over to her, "Keep your head down," but Chrissy just smiled, the sky she'd been staring at still in her eyes—a very thin, mostly invisible layer of emptiness and space.

Then Becca's mother was back, and Becca saw how her hands were shaking as she fumbled with the keys to start her car, and then they were driving away, out of the Jolly Rogers Swim Club parking lot, turning out of it into the street just as the lights and sirens tore down the whole curtain of that sunny summer day.

"Mom," Becca said.

The lights were flashing, and there were other mothers with their children now, coming out of the tunnel. There was a sun hat on the hot tar of the parking lot. There was a picnic basket that had been left beside a station wagon. There were small children crying and whining, and little boys staring in wonder at the ambulance and the men wearing uniforms, running into the tunnel through which their mothers had just pulled them. A few of them, not understanding, pointed and said, "I want to be them when I'm grown up!"

"Mom," she said again.

But her mother didn't answer.

She turned without using her signal.

Her hands looked like bones on her steering wheel.

She either didn't hear Becca, or she was hearing nothing.

"My bike," Becca said, trying to look behind her to the place she'd locked it to a rack outside the tunnel, where it would remain, locked and rusting, for at least a year before the locks on the bikes left behind that day had been removed with bolt cutters and they were taken to the dump.

She turned around in the back seat of the car and sat on her knees looking out the rearview window.

"Mom! My bike!"

"Shut up!" her mother shouted, and when Becca said it again (she couldn't help it), her mother said, "To hell with that bike!" Chrissy clapped her hands to her ears.

"Okay," Becca said. "Okay."

Her voice sounded like an older girl's

She was the older girl.

Just a little salty water squeezed out of her eyes.

Then, they were in her stepfather's driveway, and her mother turned off the car and said, without looking behind her, "Becca, go to your room right now."

Chrissy grabbed Becca's wrist then, and it hurt—her fingernails were ragged and too long—and Becca used her other hand to pry Chrissy's fingers off.

"Okay," Becca said, not crying except in a very hidden place inside her own mind, and then managing to ask her mother in a voice that surprised her, some older girl's voice, like a girl who didn't care and who knew there would be no answer to her question even as she asked it, "What did I do this time?"

"*Get away from us!*"

This time her mother shrieked it, and Chrissy started to cry, but Becca didn't even flinch. She walked up the stairs of her stepfather's house, listening as her mother tried to comfort Chrissy (*Sweetheart, I'm sorry, nothing is your fault, don't cry*) from behind her.

9

Those who were the quickest to forgive the lifeguard were those who'd attended Our Lady of the Roses with her every Sunday through all the years since her parents had moved to Mission Hills. She'd attended catechism classes with their own children. She'd gone to Sunday school. She'd performed in the annual Nativity plays—beginning as a lamb in a woolly jumpsuit that her mother made for her (using stuffing cut out of an old bedspread) and ending as the Virgin Mary, wearing a pale blue robe (a white bedsheet her mother had dyed).

Time passed, and although the lifeguard had long since left Mission Hills, her eventual growing forgiven-ness turned into gradual forgetfulness.

The Mannings, it was noted, had never been regular attendees of any church. In fact, until their son's funeral they hadn't been known to have any church affiliation whatsoever.

The lifeguard, however, had sung in the children's choir. She'd played handbells with the choir through several Advent seasons. At one Palm Sunday service, she'd performed a solo. Her voice trembled (perhaps she was thinking about her dead father), but it was lovely.

10

No one notices Richie Manning, the boy drowning in the pool that afternoon. It's the busiest day of the swim club's history. Nearly every child is in the pool. Some dive, some jump, some wait in line for the slide, some smash into the water after they've taken their turn, a few sit on the stairs to the shallow end and kick their legs so wildly that the water at their feet is churned into a hoary lather. Some of them watch the others from under the surface of the water, submerged, but with their eyes open, which was what Richie Manning most liked to do:

Swimming pool spy.

Down there it was silent except for the thumping that came from the heart inside of him, or a dulled vibration that might've been a loud bell clanging above him, but just the sound's vibration, which was a kind of ghost.

He didn't know that he was drifting. He thought he was swimming (sort of) in the shallow end. And then he was holding his breath and opening his eyes and he was *looking* . . .

He was *Swimming Pool Spy!*

Look!

Someone's twilit toes.

Someone's pale underarm.

The white sole of someone's foot.

Everything slowed down.

Down.

And down.

But then he needs to breathe, so Richie cracks up through the surface into the screams and laughter and splashing and the bright bathing suits and the chaos that had kept going on all along without him.

He can feel the sting of the chlorine in the corners of his eyes, on the roof of his mouth, that part where the bony place turns into softness, where the prickling and burning starts before it travels to the nose, moving into the dark tunnels in the skull, where the water gets in, too, sometimes, or so it had sometimes, to Richie, seemed.

Ten

10

Then he slides under again, and then he comes straight back up like a rocket blasting through the water into the sky, headed for air, all of everything that is inside him wants nothing except a breath of it, but even with his face out of the water, even surrounded by air, there are too many children today, and there isn't any air left for him.

He wheels his arms at his sides and sees that girl, the one with the bike, the one who has been here forever, the one with red hair, and he tries to say something to her, but nothing comes out of him but water.

But when the water comes out, he can breathe in the air again, and he does, puffing out his cheeks to save it. And then he's under the water. The darker part of the pool has moved closer to him. The chlorine and the aqua blue are now inside of him, and maybe that's what it is that reminds him of a summer afternoon, a million years ago, when he was his brother's age, and his grandmother was pinning sheets to a skinny rope strung between two poles in her backyard and giving him chalky peppermints.

The sheets, stark white, just bleached.

Their smell, the sky behind them.

The chemical-clean of the breeze fills him completely, and quickly, because he's so easy to fill, still a baby, each of his lungs no bigger than a newborn mouse you might find damp and alone in a nest—a tiny thing no one has noticed, would never have noticed if you hadn't.

Except—there she is:

At the bottom of the pool.

She's wearing her square pink housedress and her pockets are full of clothespins.

She's there, just under him, looking up at him, but she's standing over him, too, looking down at him, having tucked him into her laundry basket, set him out in the bleach and blue and breeze in her backyard beneath some sheets that are slapping as she forces the clothespin at one end, and then the other end, even though those sheets are so clean they want to fly away from her, so clean they don't belong to anyone.

"Oh, yes you will," she says to a sheet that doesn't want to be pinned. "Oh, yes you do," she says to a sheet that doesn't want to belong to anyone.

She's looking down at him smiling from the sky, and then she's looking up at him from the bottom of the pool, and her arms are open.

But she is deeper than he's ever been, deeper than he wants to be. He knows she's the most secret thing under the water he's ever seen, and that he's not supposed to be seeing her, even if he wants to, even though he's so happy to see her, so glad she waited for him.

But why the deep end?

Where he isn't supposed to swim.

But you aren't swimming, Richie, she says to him. *You're still learning, remember? Find a rope.*

And then Richie Manning reaches for it. It's silk. His fingers fall into it as it disappears and then he feels something hard thump his chest, and it's like the rubber tip on the end of the drumstick with feathers on it that fell off the stick.

Then he hears it at the same time he feels it.

And then the drummer punches his throat hard.

And then the drum is nothing.

9

It took me eight hours to drive from New Hampshire to Erie, Pennsylvania. The trip would have been quicker through Canada, but I was afraid that, at the border, they wouldn't accept my driver's license as proof of my identity. The photo was four years old, taken at the Chicago North Illinois Secretary of State before I started dying my hair. Before it occurred to me that anyone in the country's third largest city would recognize me as that girl from Mission Hills, the one who got raped and stabbed someone.

Although it was the same length—as short as possible—it was nowhere close to the color in the bottle that Bethany had bought for me. I thought the border guards were unlikely not to want, at least, to know what I was trying to hide. And although I'd promised myself and my sister that I wouldn't drink and drive, I knew myself well enough by then to know that by the time I got to the border I might well have something to hide.

I'd left before dawn, so it was only 2:00 p.m. by the time I exited the freeway into Erie. It was too early to check into a hotel, but I was too tired to stay safe on the freeway.

I'd promised Bethany, too, that I wouldn't drink and drive.

"Drunk drivers never die, you know. They just kill other people . . . innocent people," she'd said after taking off the plastic gloves with which she'd massaged the dye into my scalp. "Then the drivers get to live with themselves, if they can stand it, for the rest of their lives."

For whatever reason—perhaps because she was the first person in recent memory, except for Wolfie, to hold me while I cried myself to sleep—my vow to Bethany meant more to me than others I'd taken. So, I was sober.

Still, I had only stopped once, to fill up my tank at a Speedy Spot, and already by the time I crossed the sign welcoming me to

Pennsylvania, I could no longer tell if my vision was blurred or my windshield was grimy.

Erie was miles of strip malls interrupted now and then by brown, empty acreage.

At one intersection with a red light at which I had to linger for several minutes, there was time to look into one of those empty lots and watch the wind pass over the dirt to pick up a Styrofoam cup, which it launched about fifty feet into the emptiness of the sky. And that cup was still spiraling in my rearview mirror long after the light had changed, and then I was driving on until I was at a gas station, to fill up again, and to call my sister.

"Becca? Is that you? Are you in a wind tunnel or something? I can hardly hear you."

"No," I said. "I'm in Erie, Pennsylvania."

"Well, be careful. And stay sober. Mom is real worked up about how you're gonna get killed, or kill someone, on the way home."

I held the receiver away from my ear and told myself not to say anything.

I told myself that she could not be talking about that.

We did not talk about *that.*

And even if Aimee somehow no longer remembered who stabbed my stepbrother and who took the blame for it, what difference did it make to me now?

I had nowhere to go but home.

8

Once, on Christmas Eve at Trinity Lutheran, Alex thought he saw the brother he might have remembered from long ago—a boy pretending to be a shepherd in a play on the altar about Baby Jesus.

"That's him," Alex had whispered too loudly in his father's ear. When Alex leapt to his feet to see the brother better, his father grabbed his arm and pulled him back down and said, "Stop that. What are you thinking, Alex?"

Alex was thinking that he'd seen a boy he'd never seen who looked exactly like *that* boy, wearing a fake felt shepherd costume, pretending to urge a sheep across a field. The one who must be his brother.

His mother never went to church, so when Alex got home he described the boy on the altar to her and then stared closely, waiting for her reaction. He felt sure he'd know something from his mother's face when she realized what that boy might be.

But his mother pretended not to know that he was staring at her, waiting. She rolled her eyes and said, "That just sounds like Eddie Moore to me."

Alex let his held breath leave him then. Whatever it was, she wasn't going to tell him.

In truth, Marie Manning wished that the boy Alex had described sounded even slightly similar to her drowned son. But that kind of thing—visitations, apparitions—was not the kind of thing that had ever honestly happened to anyone, ever.

Lies. Delusions.

She knew all about those.

What she'd like to see was a ghost.

What she'd like to tell Alex was that his brother wasn't dead.

He lived in the attic.

Alex knew for a while that the attic was where the other boy lived.

He'd seen him, hadn't he?

Once, Alex asked his babysitter if she knew who the boy was.

"What boy?" Becca Brummler had asked.

"The one who was here before me."

Becca punched Alex (lightly) on his arm and said, "Are you seeing Brody Mansion ghosts or something?"

(The Brody Mansion was well known for its ghosts in Mission Hills, as it would continue to be for many decades before the fire, and then trespassing teenagers would claim to have seen ghosts dancing around what must once have been a fountain in the back yard.)

"No," he said. "From before that."

They were in the attic of that Brody Mansion, where Alex kept his electric train set up. It was speeding in a circle around a small town full of miniature people eating in a tiny restaurant or praying in a miniature church with electric candles burning in its windows.

"Before what?"

"There was another house," Alex said, and he started to remember it for the first time at the same time as he said it.

Another kitchen.

With checkered curtains.

A picnic basket he'd seen once, maybe, and then never again.

Many years later, after he was grown and in sales for himself and all of his mother's secrets belonged to everyone because she was dead, Alex would learn from his Aunt Pam that the timing of his brother drowning, having been the same summer that their father's income suddenly doubled, and then doubled again, made it possible for them to move straight out of that little house and into the Brody Mansion, and for his mother to go to Pine Rest while some of Richard's new secretaries from AmeriWay came to the mansion to open boxes, to pack and give away the things Mr. Manning said he never wanted to see again. He refused to list or describe these things and, instead, just said, "I trust your judgment. Just, if it's anything you think a mother in a situation like this shouldn't see," so they'd removed all the kindergartner striped shirts and plaid pajamas and rubber boots and mittens and gloves from one box and put them in another box. DONATIONS.

Obviously the Mannings wouldn't need to hand any of those clothes down to their younger son. And even if they hadn't been too rich for that, who could bear to see their younger son wearing the clothes of their other, their—drowned one?

No one!

Then the secretaries took those clothes to a Goodwill in another town, afraid that if they donated them in Mission Hills, one day Marie might be shopping and get a glimpse of some little boy, from the poor part of their town, wearing Richie's red sweater with the anchor on it, or his cap that had CHIEF embroidered on the back, RICHIE on the front.

But, as it happened, those clothes were in such good condition, and of such high quality, that they were never sold at any Goodwill after all.

They were packed up and shipped to Argentina to a consignment shop that gave Goodwill part of the profits they made selling the clothes to economy-minded mothers so that from 1969 to 1982 (maybe longer), in the mid-sized, colonial town of Salta, there was a school in which nearly every day one little boy wore a shirt, or a pair of tennis shoes, or the light summer jacket or the corduroy pants that had once belonged to the brother of Alex.

(One day in the future a local college girl who learned of this while studying abroad shared the heartwarming story with Mission Hills by writing a about it for the public library's Facebook page.)

"Well, you're the only not-ghost boy in the Brody Mansion now!" Becca had said.

Alex flipped a switch and the electric train stopped so fast a pretend apple fell out of a pile of them in a pretend box car with PRODUCE painted on its side.

7

Becca remembered feeling fear, of course, and dread, and helplessness, but she also remembered practicing something she'd seen Bruce Lee do on television. His back was turned to his enemy, who thought he was sneaking up on Bruce, believing he had an advantage, holding a knife in his hand, holding out the blade so everyone knew Bruce Lee's throat would be cut, and he would fall down in the palace and bleed to death on the beautiful floors.

Instead, just before the knife, Bruce Lee turned around, put his fists against his own chest, lifted his right foot, and kicked the creeping man in his chest. Bruce Lee's heel made a fast crack right against the man's chest, where his heart was. So the creeper grabbed his chest, fell backward onto the marble floor, blood blooming in slow motion from his cracked head—and the music then, and the fade out, and in the next scene Bruce Lee would be alive, and you knew he would stay that way.

So Becca went behind the garage and practiced over and over the swift turn (you had to be so quick that the creeper had no chance to protect himself) and then she'd kick the heel of her right foot hard against the brick wall of the garage.

At first she was clumsy. A few times the heel of her foot hurt for a week or so. But then she got faster, and better, and sometimes she could even see a dusty spot on the brick wall that was left behind by her heel. And it got more fun, too. No one could see or hear her back there, so no one asked what she was doing, and no one made fun of her when, after executing the move so smoothly she thought maybe even Bruce Lee might have congratulated her, she shouted, "Hi-YA!"

She'd never seen a Bruce Lee movie, but the boys at school talked about them so much she felt like she had.

Next, she tried to teach herself to sleep on her back, so she'd know if he had her hair wrapped around his hand and was about to yank.

But she could never sleep on her back, so she tried to stay awake.

But after all day at the pool, a sunburn on her shoulders, it was so comfortable—that princess bed her stepfather had bought for her, the window open, the sound of dusty white moths bumping into her window screen, trying to find their way to her Cinderella night light and the soft pink glow it cast over the room in the night, plugged into the electrical socket—she always fell asleep.

Then, the smell of him (some kind of spicy deodorant, pungent soap, acidic shampoo, and smoke) would wind its way into a dream.

In the dream she'd be in a witch's den, and the witches were stirring up some brew in a cauldron, which Becca imagined (trying to imagine witches eating) would be mushroom soup or oatmeal. And then one of the witches pulled her head up off the pillow, laughing (but quietly), and whispering (hot and stinky in her ear), "Hi-ho, Silver! Away we go!"

6

There was a story known to West Mission Hills Elementary School students, even to its kindergarteners, which, somehow, blessedly, no one ever told around Alex Manning.

This was a story about a swim club that had once been close to their neighborhood—close enough to ride your bike to if you were old enough to ride a bike. The pool was buried under fill dirt now, and there was an apartment complex called The Pines there (a boxy beige square around which twenty small pines had been planted, which were slowly—very slowly—growing taller). It had been a popular place to swim in the summer for several years, until the year a boy drowned in the Olympic-sized pool, and the club was closed down. (Not that anyone would have wanted to continue to belong to such a club.)

By the time anyone noticed anything wrong, that boy was lying at the bottom of the pool, just over the edge of the shallow end, in the deep end, where it dropped off into the *deep*—that spot where the water turned a shade darker, and its temperature dropped a few degrees.

It had been a busy summer day, mid-July.

A strange day, a strange summer, a strange year full of strange music, strange murders, strange clothes and hair and wars and riots:

And the moon! The rocket launch, the trip into space, the handsome astronauts and their smiling wives, and the whole country's pride and hope and fearlessness held up to them like millions of mirrors.

Although she'd been perched on a white throne above the pool, wearing special sunglasses, watching the children, watching over them, the lifeguard didn't notice the boy, drowning.

But the children were still in the pool when she started to scream, and mothers began to rush to the pool from the grassy area where they'd been lounging on the other side of a chain-link fence, to shout out their children's names, to reach down and grab them by their arms if they could, yank them out of the water before—

They saw it all:

The beautiful blond lifeguard diving into the water.

Her whistle still around her neck, floating above her, no gravity, and the old lady with the rubber flowers on her head lifting the boy before ungracefully pushing him over the side of the pool.

How old was he?

Oh, he was just a little boy—five years old or so—but his weight seemed, if you were one of the children who saw it, like the heaviest thing that had ever fallen to Earth.

Then he was tipped over by the lifeguard, and the water poured out of him.

Some children didn't get out with the others. They were confused, still fighting over a beach ball. A white towel was slipped into the pool somehow, and it was spread out in its perfect rectangle floating on the surface the whole time. Looking, obviously (everyone agreed on this) like a shroud.

While the lifeguard was kissing the boy on the mouth with her strawberry (some said wild cherry) lipgloss.

While the lifeguard—her blond hair drenched and stuck to her tanned back—was pushing on the drowned boy's chest.

A woman screamed and screamed and screamed. A baby cried. Swimmers were crawling on their hands and knees out of the water. No one would ever wait in that line to that ladder again—although, eventually, when the The Pines apartment complex was developed into the Holiday Inn Express, the top of the slide would get sheared off by the bucket of a bulldozer and then they saw there was an old pool down there, still blue.

5

The pay phone was outside the gas station, and Becca had to press the receiver of it to her ear as hard as she could to hear her sister. The freeway here ran alongside the train tracks. A long, slow train was passing by with ERIE PA painted on the side of most of the cars, which looked like they were filled with coal. Or something like coal. (Dark and prehistoric, but not heavy.) The parking lot tar under her feet buzzed.

Becca decided to just let the silence between herself and her sister surge and fade inside the telephone lines that were strung for hundreds of miles between the two of them.

"Mom said to give you her love."

"What?"

Becca didn't mean to sound so breathy and disbelieving.

But their mother had never told Becca that she loved her. It seemed unlikely she'd tell her sister.

"She's not doing that well, you know."

"Oh, that explains that then! She didn't know what she was sayin'!"

Becca laughed, but it sounded like a growl.

"Look, Becca. Not everything is about you, okay? Mom has a lot of guilt, too."

"No shit," I said.

This time I didn't bother to pretend to laugh.

What was the point?

"Well, believe it or not, she knows it. And she has a lot of—"

Silence.

My sister seemed not to remember the word for guilt.

I couldn't help but laugh then.

"What's so funny?" Aimee asked.

The train's brakes started to scream on the tracks then, and the whole thing shuddered to a stop.

"I don't know," I said. "Well, it *wasn't.* But she doesn't know that, does she?"

Mission Hills police suspect that older, not younger, sister may have stabbed the victim, despite younger's denials.

I'd liked the sound of *younger's denials.*

"Oh, or did you tell her that I confessed to murder for you?"

"Fuck you," Aimee said. "No! Because then I'd have to tell her that my sister was too stupid to keep herself from getting raped if I didn't stab somebody for her!"

"Thanks again," I said. "But I had a plan."

"Oh, shut up," Aimee said. "Your plan was to get raped."

"No, it wasn't! I wasn't going to get raped! *You're* the one who—"

"Oh, for fuck's sake, you're going to go *Thelma & Louise* on me?"

"What?"

"It's a movie. Jesus. Do you *ever* do *anything* but *drink*?"

"I quit—"

"Ha!"

"Shut up. You never—"

"You shut up. All I ever did was—"

A man seemed to be emerging from a pile of coal out of one of the train's roofless cars. Either that or he was something other than a man.

"Let's not argue," Aimee said. "Anyway, Mom wasn't talking about Davey. She was talking about that boy from the pool."

"What *boy* from the pool?"

"Seriously? You don't remember? You babysat for his brother for years. Didn't you ever wonder how you ended up babysitting for a family like the Mannings?"

Little Alex.

And the Brody Mansion with its quiet, dark rooms. Marie Manning, who stayed behind the closed door of one of them and only came out to pay me when it was time for me to go.

Mr. Manning, who was always away on business.

Maybe the richest people in West Mission Hills. We were living on the other side of Mission Hills again by then, but my mother, who wouldn't drive me two miles to Dairy Queen so I could work in the gigantic waffle cone, never begrudged the fifteen-mile drive to the Mannings.

"Mom offered your services."

"What?"

"Their son."

"*What?* I *loved* their son! I was the only one who did!"

"Oh, for God's sake, not that one. His brother. Richie Manning. You seriously don't remember? The Jolly Rogers Swim Club? Mom saw the whole thing, Becca. It wasn't your fault. He was grabbing your hair, and you—"

Yes.

Becca felt it then.

And then I—

4

All of this had happened before even the oldest of the West Mission Hills Elementary School students who'd been there that day were old enough to understand what had happened, and their brothers and sisters in kindergarten by then certainly had no memory of it.

Still, without anyone knowing how they knew, all of them knew the story and that it had to do with Alex Manning, and that they were not to tell this story around him.

It had to do with how thin and old Alex Manning's mother looked, and how sad she seemed, despite how rich her husband was and the mansion they lived in and the fancy car in which she drove Alex to school.

It was also the reason you didn't allow yourself to envy or hate Alex Manning (besides the fact that he was nice) for having everything he had, for being the only child of the richest people in a very rich place.

Once, in kindergarten, every child who knew the story inhaled sharply when Mrs. Talifero called on Alex for Show & Tell.

But she called him *Richie.*

Alex stood up then, although she hadn't called his name. He seemed, himself, surprised to be standing up after having heard another boy's name being called. But there was no one in the class named Richie, and it was his turn.

And they noticed then how Mrs. Talifero gripped the edge of her gunmetal gray desk after she said that name, seeming as if she was hanging onto it in order not to fall down, and how she started to swallow and swallow, the way you'd swallow if you had a thumbtack stuck halfway into your throat, not wanting it to come back up, but also not wanting it to go down.

Finally, she managed to say, "Alex," and she nodded at him, as if that's what she'd said the first time. "Your turn, Alex," she said.

Alex Manning showed the class a paperweight that day—a heavy solid glass bubble with a purple butterfly suspended in it.

It was his mother's.

The other kindergartners found it puzzling, maybe frightening, maybe (if they thought about it long enough) a little disgusting:

How had such a thing been caught while it was flying and trapped inside a ball of glass?

Alex Manning wanted to pass it around, but Mrs. Talifero said, "Alex." (She said his name a hundred times that afternoon, to cancel out the other name.) "That's a lovely object, and it's nice of your mother to let you bring it in, but it might be too fragile to pass around."

"My mother doesn't care," Alex said. "It's just a thing."

Mrs. Talifero didn't understand, it seemed, but the kindergartners did, and the one closest to Alex took it out of his hand, examined it briefly, and passed it to the next.

"Thank you, Alex," Mrs. Talifero said, and called on the next student, pretending for a minute that she couldn't recall Mary McNamara's name either: "Terri? Oh, I mean Mary, of course!"

Many years later, Mrs. Talifero would ask her wife, "How stupid could I be? How much stupider and sloppier could I get?"

"Are you crazy?" her wife asked. "How could you *not* make that mistake? You think about that boy all the time. And then there's his brother, who looks just like him. *Of course* you were going to slip. It must have happened to him all his life. I can't believe you only did it once."

Mrs. Talifero tuned her wife out here. She always circled around to the same thing, about which they disagreed:

"What the hell were his parents thinking, *not telling him he had a brother who drowned?* Jesus! And the whole fucking town pitched in! This place is like somewhere Shirley Jackson would think up. I said, when we left Ann Arbor, that . . ."

But Mrs. Talifero could never shake it—the way she'd not just made a terrible mistake, but had also been transported, suddenly, to the past at that moment, while standing in front of her desk in front of twenty kindergartners, looking at one of them, and seeing the one that had (*so clearly*) returned to her classroom from the dead.

When time had run backward.

When everything still had a chance.

Before anything was determined or inevitable.

That time Marie Manning ran over a nail in the road on the way to the pool, and they couldn't go to the pool, so Richie Manning had not yet drowned, and maybe never would.

If, say, that morning instead of the rocket being launched to the moon it burst into flames and fell back to Earth. And even if all three of those astronauts had to be sacrificed, Richie Manning did not have to drown.

When all three astronauts were killed as the whole country looked on in horror.

The pool didn't open that day.

Perhaps it never opened again.

The conflict in Vietnam was ended.

The country became poorer instead of richer.

Quieter instead of louder.

Kinder instead of crueler.

(Cellos and violins accompany all this.)

And no one ever stepped on the moon.

In the other universe, the one in which Richie Manning hadn't drowned, she would have simply corrected herself and never thought about it again.

But in this universe, the one in which Richie Manning existed, Mrs. Talifero would have simply corrected herself upon calling Alex Manning by his older brother's name, and she would never have thought of it again.

3

Richie Manning was halfway between the shallow end and the deep end of the pool—right around the place where they usually set out one of those rough and waxy ropes, held up by brightly colored buoys, but which they'd taken down for the swim meet that morning and had forgotten to put back.

Over his head, a string of triangular plastic flags—red, white, and blue—flapped in the breeze, while below him, the black-painted line marking the lane in which he was drowning jerked chaotically under the shifting surface of the water.

Everything else was just the jagged sunlight on a shifty mirror. The pale soles of other children's feet. Their dark and bright limbs stirring around themselves and around him, along with their colorful bathing suits, which sparked in knife blade glimpses, geometric flashes, straight into his eyeballs, not only when he surfaced, but when he slipped back under.

The edges of everything, both under and above the water, had gone sharp and hard somehow, when, usually, the world *under* the water was slowed down, in its silence, as a blur—which was what Richie Manning loved the most about the swimming pool since he first learned how to be brave enough to put his head under the water and to open his eyes, a long time ago on some other planet:

Which was the aqua blue dream of it.

Which was to actually be able to see that secret world.

When you're a secret, too.

2

The lifeguard's mother gasped when she saw that there were mealworms in her Tupperware canister of flour.

This, after all the trouble last summer with the flies.

Of course, she could have had no idea that wasps would be next.

One morning, a few months after her daughter disappeared, she'd open the basement door to a swarming horde of them.

"Oh God!" she cried out, and then she laughed at herself for crying out to God. She said, "Not you, God. You've got your hands full."

She called the exterminator, but for the rest of her life she would find tiny mummified wasps under the love seat's cushions and caught in the furnace grates.

But Mrs. Bouchelard had her faith, which she never lost.

And she was the woman in charge of organizing the receptions in the basement of Our Lady of the Roses after Sunday mass and funeral services. But she didn't want her name published in the church bulletin for this service because she didn't need anyone to know it was her. And so she went on from day to with sadness by her side, of course, but holding the Almighty's hand. She trusted that a power greater than herself was with her daughter, protecting her, too.

All of her faith was rewarded in the end, and she had all of her life's questions answered satisfactorily before she died, as the holy always do.

Also one day the lifeguard's mother went to the mailbox to find a letter in it and recognized the handwriting on the envelope addressed to her as her daughter's:

In the corner, the return address:

Julia Campion. San Francisco, California.

Dear Mom,

I'm so sorry. But please don't worry. I didn't want to tell you because I was afraid I'd change my mind . . .

So, her daughter had married him! The English teacher!

And they would stay married for thirty-two years, until Peter Campion died of a heart attack while hiking in Yellowstone Park, but not before they had three children together, all of whom grew up to be good people, and very strong swimmers, just like their mother, who was once a lifeguard.

1

AFTER THE PRESIDENT'S STATEMENT:

A clergyman should adopt the same procedure as a burial at sea, commending their souls to "the deepest of the deep," concluding with the Lord's Prayer.

Biographical Note

Laura Kasischke has published numerous novels and collections of poetry. She has been the recipient of the National Book Critics Circle Award, the Rilke Award for Poetry, a Guggenheim Fellowship, among other honors. Her work has been widely translated, and three of her novels have been made into feature-length films. She teaches at the University of Michigan, where she is the Theodore Roethke Distinguished University Professor in the Residential College.